DOWN THE LONG NIGHT

DOWN THE LONG NIGHT

WILLIAM F. NOLAN

With an Introduction by Ed Gorman

Five Star
Unity, Maine

Additional copyright information may be found on page 197.

Five Star First Edition Mystery Series.
Published in 2000 in conjunction with Tekno Books
and Ed Gorman.

Set in 11 pt. Plantin by Christina S. Huff.

Printed in the United States on permanent paper.

Library of Congress Cataloging-in-Publication Data

Nolan, William F., 1928-
    Down the long night / William F. Nolan ; with an
    introduction by Ed Gorman.
        p.   cm.
    ISBN 0-7862-2892-X (hc : alk. paper)
    1. Detective and mystery stories, American.
    2. Psychological fiction, American. I. Title.
PS3564.O39 D69 2000
  813'.54—dc21   00-061038

Table of Contents

Introduction

The first time I became aware of William F. Nolan was in November, 1963. I'm sure of the month and the year because that was when I bought his short story collection *Impact-20*, which sold for the astronomical sum of 50 cents.

The lead story in this collection (whose cover copy claimed it was "a wonderful book for all Bradbury, Serling, Hitchcock and—of course—Nolan fans") was called "The Small World of Lewis Stillman," which is about this strange, sad guy who lives underneath Los Angeles. It is one of my all-time favorite stories by anybody.

Bill Nolan, besides being a nice guy who is always helpful to young writers, is in the august company of the true literary man. Scripts for numerous "Movies of the Week." Co-author of the legendary *Logan's Run*. Writer of major biographies of Steve McQueen and Dashiell Hammett and John Huston. Twice winner of The Edgar Allan Poe award. Editor of several seminal anthologies, including his brilliant trio of Max Brand collections.

Believe me, I could go on for another two or three full pages about his accomplishments.

But the important thing is, of course, the book itself. And what a book it is. Packed full of Bill's art, talent and particular take on the human condition.

While Bill enjoys a great reputation as an important writer of fantasy-horror-science-fiction, his crime stories have been neglected. And shouldn't be.

Here is a group of crimonious tales that rank with some of the best work of the past several decades. And he's always his own man. His voice, style and attitude are all his own, particularly in the dark tales of life and death in his beloved (and sometimes despised) Southern California.

So sit back, relax, enjoy yourself. And let a master storyteller entertain and enlighten you for the next few hours.

He's one of the important ones. He really is.

—Ed Gorman

Preface

First off, I want to assure all crime buffs that this is a fresh selection. One of twelve stories I've gathered here is in print for the first time, and several others have never seen publication in book format, having been hitherto buried in now unavailable magazines. And not a single story has appeared in any of my previous collections.

I think it appropriate at this point that I lay out my basic crime credentials. I'm twice winner of the Edgar Allan Poe Special Award Scroll from the Mystery Writers of America. As a mystery-suspense writer, I've sold stories to such genre markets as *Alfred Hitchcock's Mystery Magazine*, *The Saint Detective*, *Chase*, *Mike Shane's Mystery Magazine*, *Terror Detective*, *Hard-boiled*, and *Detective Story Magazine*. I've written in the crime genre for films and television: *Melvin Purvis: G-Man*, *The Kansas City Massacre*, *Sky Heist*, and *Terror at London Bridge*. My crime fiction has been selected for such anthologies as *Best Detective Stories of the Year*, *The Year's Finest Crime and Mystery Stories*, *Dark Crimes: Great Noir Fiction*, *Murder Most Foul*, *Alfred Hitchcock Presents: The Master's Choice* and *Murder on the Aisle*.

I wrote the first book detailing the history of *Black Mask* magazine (*The Black Mask Boys*), and the first book on Hammett (*Dashiell Hammett: A Casebook*). I scripted a documentary, *Raymond Chandler's Los Angeles*, and wrote the first profile of Carroll John Daly, who pioneered the private eye in fiction. *My Hammett: A Life at the Edge* is the key biography on this author, and I also wrote the bio/critical introduction to the extensive Hammett collection from Knopf, *Nightmare*

Town. Then there's my "Black Mask Detective" series from St. Martin's Press, starring Hammett, Chandler, and Erle Stanley Gardner as crime solvers in 1930s Hollywood (*The Black Mask Murders*, *The Marble Orchard*, *Sharks Never Sleep*). I'm also the father of Private Eye Bart Challis (*Death is for Losers*, *The White Cad Cross-Up*). And, down the years, I have contributed to 35 issues of *The Armchair Detective*. Finally, in the novel I'm best known for, *Logan's Run*, the protagonist is actually a rogue cop in the future. Thus, the crime genre permeates even my work in science fiction.

Here, in *Down the Long Night*, I deal with road punks, robot detectives, and dangerous dames; with psychic investigators, comic-book crime fighters, and big-city street beggars, with deviants and drag racers—a unique mix of mayhem and murder, set in the past, present, and future.

I have provided a head note for each story, so I won't say anything more about them in this preface.

Here's my full-throttle run through a dozen wild worlds of crime.

William F. Nolan
West Hills, Calif.

"Pirate's Moon" is the first of three tales written about paranormal investigator David Kincaid. (I followed up this novelette with two Kincaid novellas, "Broxa," and "The Winchester Horror.")

I wanted to create a "new age" protagonist, breaking the mold of the Hammett-Chandler private eye. Which is to say a character who maintains an honest skepticism, but who is willing to open new doors of experience and explore unknown areas, be they natural or supernatural. (In "Broxa" he battles demonic forces, while "The Winchester Horror" is a modern day ghost story.) "Pirate's Moon" contains no demons or ghosts, but its menace is no less challenging and unexpected.

Meet David Kincaid, born in the shadow of Sam Spade and Philip Marlowe, but taken (I would like to believe) a step beyond both of them into a fresh new world of infinite possibilities.

Pirate's Moon

Although we'd never met, Dwight Robert Lee and I shared the same beach. Separated by several miles of sand, but with the same blue-green Pacific waters washing over us both. Me, wind-surfing near the Santa Monica pier, trying to forget a rough day with my tax accountant, using the ocean as personal therapy—until it got too dark and cold to stay in the water. Him, a few miles further up the coast, at Pirate's Cove, doing nothing in particular, loose-limbed, just rolling with the waves, letting them take him where they would. Neither of us was in any hurry to go anywhere.

By the time the moon came out, riding clear of a massed cloud bank, I was home, wrestling a bachelor's steak onto my backyard charcoal barbecue. Dwight Robert Lee was still at the beach. Stretched out on the cool sand in the sudden wash of moonlight. He wasn't going home that night. Not in his condition.

For one thing, his head was missing.

Naturally, I read about the discovery of his body in the *L.A. Times* the next morning. But I didn't personally get involved with the case for another week. Not until the afternoon Mike Lucero decided that he needed my help.

Mike is a close friend, so I'd better tell you about him. He's a homicide detective working out of the Malibu Sheriff's Station. Built like a weight lifter. Big, slab-muscled, with a wide grin that buries his eyes in sun wrinkles. Miguel Francisco Lucero. Oldest of nine children. He grew up on one of those small mountain villages in northern New Mexico where they believe in witches and mal *ojo,* the evil eye. (Helps him put up with me!) After he left the University of New Mexico with a degree in psychology, he headed for California. Wanted to be a cop. And since there's always a need for bilingual officers in the L.A. County Sheriff's Department, Mike got signed up fast.

He lives in Woodland Hills, in the western San Fernando Valley, with his wife, Carla, and a loud pair of twin five-year-old daughters. He's a good man and a good detective.

I met Mike three years ago, when he attended one of my psychic seminars. As a cop, he figured it would help if he could develop his psychic ability. We all have it, to one degree or another. Some more, some less. Just a matter of self-development. I'm into the world of the paranormal; it's what I do for a living. I teach, write, investigate, conduct seminars, hold personal consultations—the works. I don't expect everybody to believe in all the stuff I deal with (I'm still mentally struggling with a lot of it myself), but I do ask people to keep an open mind about our incredible universe and what might or might not be in it. In outer *and* inner space—the space inside our being. You, me, and the cosmic universe. A big package.

Anyhow, after listening to some of my ideas, Mike figured I was a certified nut case and we didn't see each other again for a year. Until the body of a teenage girl was found in Topanga Canyon with her throat cut. No clues. No suspects.

Mike came to me, reluctantly, and asked if I could help him crack the case. Brought along a ring found on the body. "You're the psychic," he growled, "so tell me what happened."

I couldn't. My psychic powers are quite limited. I sent him to a woman named Brenner in Pasadena. She "read" the dead girl's ring, and her mental visions eventually led Mike to the killer. Doesn't always work that way, but this time it did. Lucero was impressed.

We talked. Had dinner together. By evening's end, he gave me that slit-eyed grin of his and said, "Damn if I don't think we're friends. What do you think?"

Over the next two years I helped Mike on half a dozen cases. Not all of them were solved, but I gave each one my best shot. Which is why I'm an official Sheriff's Consultant— with a shiny badge to prove it.

So here was big Mike Lucero, on a foggy coastal afternoon in May, sprawled across my living-room couch, sipping from a can of Diet Pepsi, talking about the dead man found under a pirate's moon.

"This guy was one bad dude," Mike declared. "They called him Stomper. That's because he enjoyed putting the boot to people he mugged." Mike took a swig from his Pepsi. "Dwight Robert 'Stomper' Lee. A sick-minded sadistic shit. Believe me, he was no loss to society."

I was across the room in a chair by the fireplace. Wasn't fire weather; it's just my best chair. "How come you know his name when the corpse was stripped and his head was missing? How'd you make the ID?"

"Body tattoo. Skull and crossbones on the right side of his chest. Which told us he belonged to the Henchmen."

"That outlaw cycle gang?"

"Right. Every member of the Devil's Henchmen has to carry a chest tattoo."

"Even their women?"

"You bet. On the right tit. Anyhow, we figured he'd have a record and ran his prints. Bingo. Computer told us all we wanted to know about him."

"Except who killed him."

"Yeah." Mike nodded. "Not that I personally give a damn. Whoever did it rates a medal—but I happen to be a cop and he happens to be a murder victim. So you play the game." Mike shrugged his heavy shoulders.

"Why come to me on this one?" I asked him.

"Because we're zip on it. Absolute dead-end. And because it's weird." He gave me his slitted grin. "You know I always bring the weirdos to you, Dave."

"So what's so weird about finding a cycle freak with his head missing? Maybe he ripped off another Henchman's chick and they stomped the Stomper. Or it could be the work of a rival gang who kept his head for a souvenir."

"Whoever did it took more than his head," said Mike.

I raised an eyebrow. "More?"

"The scumbag's heart was missing. Cut right out of the body." Mike reached into his jacket and handed me an object

14

sealed in clear plastic—a beaded feather, with a complex pattern of bright threads wound through it. "We found this at the beach near Lee's corpse. You know something about Indians, so I brought it here."

I'd told Mike a lot about my childhood—about my early years in Arizona on the Hopi Reservation. My parents worked there for the U.S. Bureau of Indian Affairs. After they died—in a desert flash flood when I was six—I grew close to an old, half-blind Hopi medicine man who became a father figure to me. He gave me my first real taste of the spiritual world when he taught me the metaphysical Hopi view of life. Later, at the University of Arizona, I expanded my knowledge by studying Indian lore from a wide variety of tribes.

So Mike was right. I know something about Indians. I carefully examined the feather, turning it slowly in the air.

"Well?" Mike growled impatiently. "What tribe is it from?"

"None," I said.

"Huh?"

"I mean it's not from any Indian tribe in North America."

"Where then?"

"You got me. I've never seen one like it. How do you know this is connected with Lee's murder?"

"I don't," Mike admitted. "It could have washed up on the beach the same way he did."

"Have you tried a psychic?"

"Sure, a couple. The two you put me onto—the Brenner woman and that bearded guy in Santa Monica, Dorfman."

"What did they tell you?"

"A lot of nothing is what they told me." He scowled, scrubbing a hand along his cheek. "Claimed they couldn't get any kind of clear reading on it."

"Then maybe the feather's *not* related to Lee's death," I said, handing it back. "Could have been tossed into the ocean by anybody."

"Yeah." Mike sighed. "Who the hell knows?"

He put his empty soda can on the coffee table and stood up. "Well, thanks anyhow."

"Going already?"

"Have to. Carla's got dinner in the microwave. I promised her I'd be home early."

"Tell her I said hi."

"Sure." When he reached the door he turned to level a hard look at me. "When you gonna get married again?"

"Whoa, pal! Give me some time. The divorce papers have barely cooled."

"Don't shit me," growled Mike. "You need a woman. Living alone is no damn good."

And he was gone before I could think of a snappy reply to that one.

A month later, in late June, Lucero contacted me again. I'd been out of state, conducting a mind-expansion seminar outdoors in Arizona, and I got back to find Mike's recorded growl on my answering machine. His message was brief and to the point: "Another murder. And another damn feather. Call me."

When I reached him by phone at the station he seemed edgy. " 'Bout time you got back. Where the hell were you?"

"In the Arizona desert earning my living," I said tersely. "You know, I'm not paid to be on call to the Malibu Sheriff's Department."

His tone softened. "Okay, okay . . . I'm out of line. But this has been a crappy week."

I eased back on the couch, the receiver cradled against my shoulder. "So tell me about the second feather."

"I'd rather show it to you. Can you come down to the station?"

"I guess so."

"Then I'll be waiting." And he rang off.

★ ★ ★ ★ ★

The ocean sun was laying its usual late-afternoon strips of hammered gold over the surface of the Pacific when I turned off the Coast Highway and rolled my little red CRX Honda into the parking area at the Malibu station.

Mike looked sour and angry when I walked into his office. Obviously, the case was at a standstill. He nodded toward a battered leather chair facing his desk. I took it.

"How'd your outdoor seminar go?"

"Could have been better. It rained both days."

"Manage to expand any females?"

"Is that supposed to be funny?"

"Just friendly concern."

Mike settled behind his work-cluttered desk, a scarred oak relic that looked like a thrift-shop reject. In fact, Mike's office was something less than sumptuous. It smelled of mildewed files and stale cigar smoke. But he'd fought a lot of wars here and wasn't about to change anything.

I put out a hand. "Let me see it."

He gave me the second plastic-sealed feather. It was almost identical to the first. Bright with beads and intricately threaded.

"What about the body?" I asked.

"Same MO. Head missing. Heart cut out."

"Tattoo on his chest?"

"No. This guy was no scummy biker. He was a real celebrity. Athlete. Olympic runner. Had his picture on the cover of *People* last month. They called him the California Iron Man."

"Eddie Lansdale?"

"Yeah, him." Mike took a cigar from his desk and ran a match flame carefully around the tip. "He was easy to identify. Had a missing thumb on his right hand. Born that way." He let out a deep sigh. "The newspapers are gonna have a field day with this one."

"Where was he found?"

"Santa Monica Mountains. Couple of honeymooners were backpacking into the area when their mutt ran into this cave and began digging like crazy. Lansdale was buried there—*with* the feather. We still don't know what the hell it means."

His cigar had gone out and he was running a fresh flame over it.

"I'd like to take both feathers to someone I know. An anthropologist. He might be able to help." I looked at Mike. "What do you say?"

"I say they're the only clues we've got. I'm not supposed to let them out of my sight." He hesitated. "But go ahead, *take* the damn things. See what you can find out about 'em."

He opened his desk again and gave me the other feather.

"I'll be careful with your only clues," I said.

Mike grunted. He was still looking sour when I left his office. But at least he had his cigar going.

On-campus parking at UCLA is usually a hassle, but I got the CRX stashed neatly on a lot close to my target: Haines Hall. Home of Sidwick Sims Oliver, B.A., M.A., Ph.D. And the chairman of the Department of Anthropology.

Sid looked more like a Texas linebacker than a university professor, with his wide shoulders and bulky torso, but a pair of thick-lensed tortoiseshell glasses testified to his bookish character.

"Kincaid! Happy to see you!" He greeted me in his usual expansive manner with a crushing bear hug. (He never called me David.) Then he stepped back, frowning. "My God, are you trying out for Wild Bill Hickok?"

He referred to my fringed-buckskin shirt, Levi's, silver Indian belt, and tooled-leather boots.

"I'm a desert critter, remember? Sun and sand and cacti. Haven't been in a suit since my Uncle Jack was buried. And that was three years ago."

Sid chuckled, a bass rumble. "To each his own!"

We were standing in the hall, flanked by shelves of native artifacts from a dozen world cultures. He waved me into his office. Which was as neat as he was. A place for everything and everything in its place. With all his papers in neat little piles. Freud would have called him anal retentive.

"I need your expertise," I told him as Sid handed me a minicarton of fresh carrot juice from his office fridge. He selected mango juice for himself. We sat down facing one another.

"You helping the police on another case?"

I nodded. "Yeah. The Sheriff's Department. This one involves two headless corpses found in the Malibu area."

"Two!" Sid pursed his thick lips. "I read about the headless cycle gentleman. But . . . *another!*"

"It'll be in the papers by tonight," I said. "With all the gory details. Well . . ." I corrected myself. "Not *all* the details. It won't mention these."

And I produced the two feathers.

He took the plastic-covered objects gingerly into his large hands, peering myopically. The sun from the window fired the beads to points of brightness.

I leaned toward him. "Can you identify them?"

"Of course I can," he said, raising his head to me. "They're from Papua New Guinea. The threading and the beads are ceremonial. Stone Age stuff."

I blinked at him. "What are feathers from the Stone Age doing next to dead bodies in Malibu?"

"I didn't say they were actually *from* the Stone Age," Oliver grumbled. "It is simply that tribal customs in New Guinea have remained constant since that era. As to their connection with your two corpses, that is up to you and your police friends to determine."

"Can you tell me what specific tribe these are from?"

"No. That would be extremely difficult for me to ascertain. I'm no expert on New Guinea. But I know someone who is."

"Here in the department?"

He shook his head. "A freelance professional journalist. Kelly Rourke's done research in the mountains of Papua. You could talk to Rourke."

"Sounds good."

Oliver flipped through the cards in his Rolodex, scribbled on a notepad, tore off the page, and handed it to me. "Rourke has an apartment in the American Comic Book Company building on Ventura. That's Studio City."

I scanned the note page. "Phone?"

"No, Rourke hates phones. Just go on over. Say I sent you. Odds are you'll get your information."

"Sid . . ." I clapped him on the shoulder. "I owe you a lunch."

"Solve the case and we'll celebrate. You can buy me champagne."

"For *lunch?*"

"Brunch. A champagne brunch."

And I had to submit to another crushing bear hug before I got out of there.

I took Sunset from UCLA, passing all the giant showbiz billboards along the Strip, gaudily promoting rock groups with names like Shiva, Orange Love, and The Little Big Men, then turned left on Laurel Canyon and made my way up and over the twisting snake of road that divides Hollywood from the San Fernando Valley. The little CRX danced through the curves like a prima ballerina and I got to Ventura Boulevard in jig time.

The American Comic Book Company was on the second floor. I climbed the carpeted steps, with a jagged red lightning bolt painted on the wall, to a wide landing with two doors facing one another. The first was open, and I peered into a comic fiend's paradise. Wall-to-wall superheroes in multicolored underwear.

The second door was closed. On pebbled glass, lettered in black, were the bold words: GO AWAY. I DON'T LIKE STRANGERS. AND IF YOU'RE SELLING ANY-THING—DIE!

I hoped Sid was right about my getting cooperation. Mr. Rourke didn't seem the friendly type.

I rapped on the glass. A red-haired knockout in a tight black turtleneck and thigh-hugging plum stretch pants opened the door and glared at me. "Can't you *read?*"

"Must have the wrong office," I said. "I'm looking for Mr. Rourke. He's a writer."

"You're looking at him," she said. "Only I'm a *her*."

"You certainly are," I said.

She smiled at my lewd enthusiasm. "My mother's maiden name was Kelly. She planned on giving it to her son, but I came along instead. I'm always surprising people."

"You sure surprised me," I admitted. "I'm David Kincaid. Sid Oliver sent me here. He said I should talk to you."

"About what?"

"A double murder that may extend back to the Stone Age."

That one got me inside.

". . . and when I needed more data, Sid suggested you. So here I am."

"Let's see the feathers," she said.

I gave them to her. Their glowing colors contrasted with the dimness of the room. Kelly told me she kept the curtains drawn because she could think better that way; raw sunlight bothered her when she was writing. Well, as Sid would say, to each his own.

Her place was neat and comfortable. Big-pillowed sofas (we were sitting on one), antique chairs, oil paintings of ocean sunsets, and a cabinet of painted plates behind glass. Plus books. Lots of books. Writers have books like alley cats have fleas. Comes with the territory.

After she'd examined the feathers, Kelly walked to a shelf, selected one of the books, brought it over to me. The title was in red: *Tribal Customs of Papua New Guinea*. By Nigel somebody.

"New Guinea's part of Australia, isn't it?" I asked.

"Used to be, but they got their independence in 1975." She flipped the book open. "Look at these."

The photos were in full color, showing gaudily painted natives with bones through their noses jumping up and down inside a big bamboo hut of some kind. And they all wore feathers.

"That's a Purari ceremonial dance," said Kelly. "The masked dancers in red and black represent ghosts of the dead, and that tall character, the really ugly one in the middle, he's a witch doctor. Chases away evil spirits. Check the feathers he's wearing."

She placed one of Mike's murder clues next to a close-up photo in the book. "Notice the pattern—the way the beads are threaded into the main body of the feather."

"Yeah . . . they're the same."

"And your missing heads and hearts tie right in."

"To what?"

"To their tribal customs." She gave me a steady look, "The Purari were cannibals."

I let out a long breath as Kelly continued.

"They severed the heads for luck. Or what *we'd* call luck. Sleeping on a skull at night was considered strong magic."

"And the hearts?"

"They devoured them. In order to absorb the victim's *mana,* or life force. Eating the heart was supposed to give them the victim's strength."

I leaned back into the pillow, turning one of the feathers slowly in my right hand.

"Could these be fake? I mean, not the real McCoy?"

"Nope," Kelly said flatly. "For one thing, the thread pattern is far too subtle and complex."

"Meaning what?"

"Meaning that only a real Papua New Guinean would know how to make these. Most likely a tribal witch doctor."

"We don't have cannibal witch doctors in L.A.," I said.

"They don't have them in New Guinea, either. Not anymore. Cannibalism has been extinct there for a long time."

"Then how do you explain all this?"

"I don't. But I think we should go talk to the Australian consul general."

"We?"

"As a writer, I want to follow through on this. Might get a piece for *The New Yorker* out of it. Okay with you?"

"I never say no to a beautiful woman."

Kelly smiled sweetly. "Bullshit," she said.

The abstract stained-glass tower of St. Basil's Cathedral speared its long shadow across Wilshire Boulevard, darkening the marbled entrance court of Paramount Plaza. Kelly and I walked through the tall doors of an elegant twenty-story stone-and-black-glass office building and took the elevator to the seventeenth floor.

Above an impressive continental shield, featuring an embossed kangaroo, the words AUSTRALIAN CONSULATE GENERAL were gold-leafed on the door of Suite 1742.

We went in. Several pale orange couch chairs faced a wall of shelved reference books. A framed painting of Queen Elizabeth II, in royal regalia, was on the wall next to a large contour map of Australia.

Kelly walked over to a stiff-faced lady in a glass-fronted reception booth and told her we were here to see the man himself, Sir Leslie Fraser-Shaw.

"Do you have an appointment with Sir Leslie?"

"I called in. He knows me. He's agreed to see us."

The stiff-faced receptionist verified this on her intercom, then ushered us into the sanctum sanctorum.

As we entered, Fraser-Shaw rose like a white-suited Buddha from a desk the size of a polished iceberg. He was a wide-bodied man in his sixties, with a florid complexion and deeply pouched eyes. He gave us a political smile.

"Ah, Kelly, my dear . . . safely back from the untrammeled wilds of Mongolia, I see."

"Yep, two weeks ago," she said.

"Splendid!" Fraser-Shaw swung his puffy eyes in my direction. "And you are . . . ?"

"David Kincaid. From the untrammeled wilds of Malibu."

"Ah, yes." His smile wavered. He led us to a long white sofa. "Please make yourselves comfortable."

Sir Leslie settled down next to us, folding his small pink hands across the bulk of his stomach.

"Now, my dear," he said to Kelly, "just how may I be of service to you? Planning another Australian trip?"

"No, not this time," she said. "Mr. Kincaid is assisting the police on a homicide. Two of them, in fact. The murders may involve tribal Papua."

"How very peculiar," said Fraser-Shaw.

"Our purpose in coming here," I said, "is to find out what you can tell us about people from Papua New Guinea who may now be living in the Los Angeles area."

"This is the *Australian* Consulate," Sir Leslie said firmly. "We have no legal ties to Papua New Guinea."

"I realize that—but since there is no New Guinea consulate . . ."

Fraser-Shaw shifted in his chair, tenting his delicate pink fingers. "Of course there are many Australians here in Southern California, but I really don't believe there are any residents from Papua New Guinea. At least, not to my knowledge."

"There was a ceremonial feather left at the site of each murder," I said. "From Papua."

"They're definitely authentic tribal feathers," Kelly declared. "Very much the real thing."

"Your murderer could be a collector," said Fraser-Shaw. "He could have purchased the feathers in Papua—leaving them as, one might say, his personal calling cards."

"That's possible," I admitted.

Sir Leslie checked his watch and stood up, letting us know the meeting had ended.

"I do wish I could spend more time discussing this matter with you," he said, "but I am victim to a crowded schedule."

"Appreciate your seeing us, Sir Leslie," said Kelly, smiling at him.

He put a fleshy paw on her shoulder. "You are most welcome, my dear. And if I can be of any further help, do not hesitate to call on me."

"We just might do that," I said.

He nodded toward me. "Good luck with your inquiries, Mr. Kincaid."

I said thanks to that.

After a late dinner, I dropped Kelly off at her comic-book

address, promising to "keep her in the picture" as the case progressed—*if* it progressed. Then I phoned Mike Lucero and filled him in on the Papua New Guinea angle. He was, to say the least, highly skeptical about the possibility of Stone Age cannibals in Los Angeles.

"But it explains the feathers," I told him.

"Sure it does," he said. "Now all we have to do is find a *real* explanation. Just bring 'em back to me in the morning, okay?"

"In the morning," I said.

I drove home under a full moon, turning off Malibu Canyon Road at Las Virgenes and aiming the CRX up the mile-long climb past the Hindu Temple to road's end near the Cottontail Ranch. I eased the Honda down the curving gravel drive fronting my place, got out, and took a deep breath—inhaling the sweet scent of pine, sage, and oleander. And even this far inland a sea wind brought me the faint iodine smell of the Pacific. There are worse places to live, and I was smiling as I keyed open the front door.

Inside, I experienced a neck-prickling sensation that told me I wasn't alone.

I spun from the door as three tall, heavily muscled figures came for me, brandishing wicked looking knives and spears. They had bones in their noses. The moonlight played across naked chests and painted faces, and all I could think of was how goddam surprised Mike Lucero would be to see his ole buddy being attacked at home by three frothing Stone Age cannibals.

I dropped into a defensive crouch as a bamboo spear whistled past my left ear to bury itself in the wall. I figured it was time to make all those painful hours of karate practice pay off.

I took out the first guy with a *yoko-geri*—a powerful side kick to the neck with the outside edge of my right boot. He went down like chopped timber.

I pivoted toward the second guy, into a *mawashi-zuki,* thrusting my left fist forward in a roundhouse half-circle from the hip to the side of his head. He crashed backward, taking a lamp table down with him.

The third guy was the biggest, with a long raised scar puckering his right cheek, and he was charging in with a raised blade big enough to impress Jim Bowie. I ducked under the glittering arc of his knife and put the elbow of my right arm hard into his ribs, the always-effective *empi-uchi.* One of his bones cracked, like a dry twig breaking. He grunted and dropped the knife, staggering, his eyes wild, lips pulled back from the pain.

I was gearing up for more action when the three of them decided they didn't like my magic. The knife-wielder scooped up his blade and the spear-thrower retrieved his spear. Then, like three night shadows, they left the way they'd come in, sliding through the living-room window and instantly vanishing into the thick brush and trees.

When Mike Lucero answered the phone his opening words were fogged with sleep. "Yeah . . . who . . . who's calling?"

"Kincaid."

"*Dave?* Christ, it's late! Don't you ever go to bed?"

"Being attacked by cannibals tends to keep me awake."

He was really pissed now. "You call me in the middle of the friggin' night because you're having a friggin' dream about cannibals?"

"No dream, Mike. These three boys were the genuine article. Feathers, body paint, bones in the nose—like they stepped right out of a Stone Age time machine."

"I thought you didn't do drugs," Mike growled.

Now *I* was pissed and allowed the anger to edge my voice. "I

27

don't, and you know it. I'm telling you straight. When I got home tonight three painted savages with knives and spears were waiting for me. They damn well tried to *kill* me. Without my karate training I would have bought the farm."

"Okay, okay . . . I'll take your word about the attack. But whoever they were, they weren't Stone Age savages."

"Who were they then?"

"Could've been three of the Henchmen, playing native. To go with the feathers they planted on the two bodies. Trying to freak you off the case."

"You think the Henchmen are responsible for both murders?"

"I'm not ruling out the idea. I questioned as many of those slimeballs as I could round up—and they're a mean bunch of mothers, lemme tellya. They could be using all this New Guinea savage crap as a smokescreen."

"But *why?* What's the point of it all? If they wanted to snuff the Stomper and the Olympic guy for some reason, why not just kill them outright, with no frills? Why the big masquerade?"

"Could be their sick sense of humor. These people are *twisted*, Dave."

"I don't buy it," I said firmly. "It's just too bizarre."

"Look." Mike sighed. "Let's talk at the station. I gotta get back to sleep or I won't be worth shit tomorrow. I'm just glad you're okay." He hesitated. "You *are* okay, right?"

"I'm fine. Not a scratch."

"Then can we talk about this in the morning? You can file a full report."

"Sure. In the morning."

And I rang off.

When I woke at ten, the sun was hiding out. A fog had blown in from the ocean, making everything gray and cobwebby. Which was how I felt. I showered, dressed, and fixed myself Swedish pancakes for breakfast. Whenever I get depressed I treat myself to Swedish pancakes. Stomach therapy.

I was in no hurry to talk to Mike Lucero. We'd said all there was to say at this point, and I figured I'd rather look into Kelly's deep green eyes than Mike's scowling cop's mug. So I phoned her.

She seemed delighted to hear from me. "I was going to call *you*," she said. "I want to take you someplace special today. To see a bloke I know."

"A *bloke?* That's Aussie talk."

"It's the only clue I'll give you," she said. And she laughed.

Forty-five minutes later I picked her up in front of her comic-book building in Studio City and asked where we were headed.

"For Yuppie Heaven," she said. And her green eyes glinted.

I knew where that was: the oh-so-hip area of neoned "in" shops and cafés stretching for several blocks along Melrose, below Hollywood. With names like the Last Wound-up, Indiana Joan's, and the Big Bravo. Where all the young, upwardly mobile couples twitter over the latest craze in clothes, videos, records, collectibles, and books.

On the way over I told Kelly about my violent brush with the Stone Age. She was shocked when she realized I wasn't kidding.

"Mike figures they were cycle freaks, coming on as natives," I said.

"He's wrong," Kelly declared. "From your description, I'd say they were real."

"Real *savages?*"

"Not in the sense one associates with the term. But definitely people from Papua New Guinea."

"But Fraser-Shaw told us there aren't any people from New Guinea in L.A."

"He said he didn't *know* of any. Well, I do."

"Yesterday you didn't."

"That was then and this is now. I did some phoning. That's why we're going where we're going. You'll see."

"Okay, but I'm running out of patience. Where the hell *are* we going?"

"The Down-Under," said Kelly.

The place is owned by a female pop singer from Australia. When you go inside there are dozens of framed pictures of her along the walls. And near the back there's this big screen with constantly running footage of her performing but with no sound-track. It's kind of spooky, watching her sing with no words coming out.

"It wouldn't be appropriate to our overall atmosphere."

That's what the manager of Down-Under told me when I asked him why we couldn't hear the singer singing. He was the Aussie "bloke" Kelly had taken me to meet. Derek Newcombe, a tall string bean of a guy. Seems his parents used to work with the natives in Papua New Guinea before the big split with Australia.

He was standing behind the planed-wood "Aussie Milk Bar" (in red neon letters) as Kelly and I perched on two high stools at the counter.

"What'll it be, mates?" Derek asked.

"Vegemite, and a Blue Heaven milk shake." Said Kelly.

"I'll just go with the Blue Heaven," I said. And turned to her. "What's Vegemite?'

"It's great! Everybody in Australia has it for breakfast. Highly nutritious, too."

When her order arrived, with the Vegemite spread darkly over buttered wheat, it looked exactly like cinnamon toast. And I *love* cinnamon toast.

"Want a bite?" she asked.

"You bet," I said.

"Chew it thoroughly," advised Derek.

I bit into Vegemite-covered toast and began chewing. "Gah!" I sputtered, barely able to swallow the stuff.

"I don't think he cares for it," Derek said to Kelly.

She nodded. "It's an acquired taste." And she dug into her order with sickening enthusiasm.

"What the hell's it *made* of?"

"Yeast, mainly."

"Yech! No wonder."

Two big stuffed kangaroos flanked the bar, and I would rather have bitten into one of them.

Then Kelly got to the point of our visit.

"Derek, on the phone this morning, you told me that you know for a fact that there are at least two to three dozen people from Papua New Guinea living in the Los Angeles area. We've come here to find out about them."

Newcombe compressed his lips and scratched his head, looking like Stan Laurel. And he also had Laurel's sad eyes. "Well . . . maybe I spoke out of turn."

"What's that supposed to mean?" I asked him.

"These people . . . they're very private. Keep to themselves. They don't like to mix with outsiders."

I nodded. "With anyone who isn't from Papua New Guinea, you mean?"

"Right, mate. Exactly right." He even had Laurel's high, piping voice—but with a thick Aussie accent. "I wouldn't advise attempting to make contact with any of them. If that's what you had in mind."

"Really?" I said. "Well, three of 'em sure tried to make contact with *me* last night."

"I don't follow you, mate," said Derek.

"Forget it," I said. "Just tell us where we can find these people."

"I'm not sure . . . if I should . . ." Newcombe looked uncertain.

"C'mon, Derek, what's the problem?" Kelly demanded. "We just need to ask them a few questions. It's no big deal."

"All right then, luv," said Newcombe. "Go down to Third and San Pedro. There's a bar on the corner—the Imunu. That's where they congregate. Kind of a meeting place for them."

"How do we know when they'll be there?" I asked. "Or what they look like?"

"My father goes there to drink with them sometimes," said Newcombe. "He told me that this tall bloke from Papua named Dibela works there days as a bartender. He might answer whatever questions you have. But I wouldn't count on it."

"How do we recognize Dibela?" asked Kelly.

"That's easy. Bloke has a right fierce scar along his cheek."

I did a double take on that one. Jackpot! The spear-thrower!

It was time to move.

"Thanks, mate," I said, steering Kelly toward the door. She was still nibbling Vegemite on the way. "Be sure to give Olivia our best next time you see her."

When we left, the singer was still performing soundlessly on the screen.

I phoned Mike Lucero and told him to meet me at the Imunu in an hour and that I'd explain why when he got there. Then we took the Hollywood Freeway into central L.A. I parked the CRX in a lot a half-block east of the bar. The afternoon sun was gradually sliding down the edge of the western sky, lengthening our shadows as we moved along San Pedro.

Walking through this seedy, down-at-the-heels area, passing the battered, grimed storefronts, decorated by dopers, winos, grifters, pimps, and prostitutes, was a depressing business. This was another, darker world, full of poverty and violence and smashed lives. Derek had it right; we didn't belong here.

The Imunu was a typical product of the area. A soot-blackened COORS sign flickered in dying neon behind a grease-filmed window. The bar's name had been painted on a strip of peeling wood above the front door, but the last two letters had flaked away, leaving only IMU on the weathered board.

Inside, the air reeked of sour tobacco and spilled beer. "This place would give Count Dracula the creeps," I muttered to Kelly.

It wasn't crowded. Perhaps a dozen drinkers huddled over their glasses at tables and booths, regarding us with suspicious eyes as we crossed the smoke-dimmed room to the bar.

"Shouldn't we wait for your cop friend?" Kelly asked me. I'd told her about the scar. "This Dibela guy might go for you again."

"Not in public," I said. "And not without his pals. I just want to make sure he's the same bird before Mike gets here to put the cuffs on him."

"Okay." Kelly shrugged. "We'll play it your way."

The guy behind the bar was tall and black and mean-looking, but he *didn't* have a scar on his cheek.

"What you want?" he demanded, with a glare.

"Does a man named Dibela work here?" I asked.

"Maybe."

I slid a ten-dollar bill across the counter. He closed his hand over it like a shark's jaw, not looking at the money. He kept glaring at me.

I waited. "Well?"

33

"He took off early today—couple of minutes before you came in. Said he had something special he had to do. Might still be able to catch him." The bartender flicked his head toward the rear of the building in a quick gesture. "Got an old Ford pickup truck. Keeps it round back. If it's there, he's there."

"Thanks," I said, and hustled outside with Kelly. We sprinted for the lot behind the building. Dibela was just getting into the pickup—rusted-orange, with dented fenders and the rear bumper missing. We got a side flash of his scarred face as he climbed into the truck.

"Is that the guy?" asked Kelly.

"Yep. Only his spear is missing." I looked around, the muscles in my jaw tightening. "Where the hell's Lucero? Guy's gonna be long gone in another two seconds!"

Then Mike's unmarked car rolled up to us. Talk about the nick of time! He waved from the window. "Saw you hop around the building. What's going down?"

I climbed into Mike's car, pulling Kelly in after me. I'd introduce them later. "See that guy in the Ford?"

It passed us, pulling onto San Pedro.

"Yeah, so what?"

"So follow him—but don't let him know he's picked up a tail. He's one of the three weirdos who attacked me. I figure he could lead us to the others."

"You've been a busy little bee since last night," Mike declared, moving out into the traffic flow.

"You packing your .38?" I asked.

He patted his coat. "Always."

"Good. We just might need it."

Dibela had no idea he was being tailed, but Mike was careful anyhow, staying far enough back to keep out of his driving mirror. Our boy cleared downtown L.A. and got on the Ventura Freeway, with us right behind him.

As we drove I told Mike all about Kelly and Derek New-combe and filled in details of the night attack.

"And you're a hundred percent sure the guy we're after was one of them?" he asked.

"Hundred percent," I said. And told them about the scar.

He nodded, smiling faintly. It was the kind of smile I'd seen on his face before, when a tough case was coming into focus. "Sounds like you two are really on to something."

Kelly leaned toward him. "Then you're ready to believe us now—about the New Guinea tie-in to the murders?"

"I'd be a fool not to, at this point," he said. "Wacko as it seems, you've got me convinced we're chasing a goddam cannibal down the Ventura Freeway!"

And we all grinned.

Dibela took the off ramp for Malibu Canyon Road, heading toward the coast. He didn't give any indication he'd seen us as Mike made the same turn, three cars behind the pickup.

The road twisted through rolling hills the color of lion pelts, with the lowering sun tinting the distant horizon.

"When you didn't show up at the station this morning, I began feeling guilty," Mike said.

I looked at him. "Why guilty?"

"The way I put you off last night, right after you'd practically been killed. As if my getting some extra shut-eye was more important than what you had to tell me."

"Hey, Mike, there was nothing you could have done. I just wanted you to know what happened."

"I still feel guilty about it. Then today, when you didn't show or call in, I began to worry—that maybe those three creeps had come back for you. So I drove over to your place to check it out. When you didn't answer, I forced a window to get inside, but you were gone."

"I meant to call you earlier, but Kelly took me under her wing."

"I have very soft feathers," she said.

Mike chuckled deep in his throat. "Seems you two make a good team. And if I do say so, a damn handsome couple."

I could see where this was heading, with Mike Cupid trying to set up a new soulmate for his ole buddy Dave. Another ten miles and he'd have us married.

The road now sliced between Malibu Canyon's sheer walls, with steeply rising sun-shadowed cliffs of tumbled granite to our left. California can look like many states, and right now it looked like the canyon country of Arizona. Hard to believe, at this moment, that a big blue ocean was waiting just over the ridge.

There was only one car between us and the Ford pickup when Dibela swung abruptly off the highway onto a narrow dirt trail leading into the mountains. The sudden route change took Mike by surprise, and we skidded over some rough ground before reversing to complete the turn. By then the Ford was out of sight around a twist in the trail.

"This is no road," Mike grumbled. "Where the hell's he *going?*" He lifted his head, eyes slitted against the sky. "Nothin' up there but trees and rock. It's all raw wilderness."

"You found the second body in the mountains," I reminded him. "Maybe these New Guinea boys have some kind of headquarters up here."

"Makes sense," said Kelly. "This terrain is a lot like the mountains of Papua. Probably makes them feel right at home."

The dirt trail looped and bumped us upward, full of deep cuts and half-buried stones. Fit for coyotes, not cars. We were following the Ford's dust cloud, so there was no way Dibela could spot us behind him.

When the dust thinned, Mike slowed to a crawl, knowing Dibela had stopped somewhere just ahead. He drove off the trail into heavy chaparral, shielding the car.

"We walk from here," Mike said. "Stay right behind me, and keep to the trees. We don't want to be seen." He slipped the .38 from its clamshell holster, checked the load. "No telling what we'll run into."

With Mike leading, we proceeded cautiously through the trees paralleling the dirt trail. The sun had now dropped below the horizon, and an early-evening chill, blown in from the ocean, was settling over the mountains. We were moving through scented stands of eucalyptus, oak, and sycamore. There were king snakes and rattlers in these mountains, and I hoped we wouldn't be stepping on any. Or on a mountain lion's tail.

"You okay?" I asked Kelly.

"Sure." She nodded. Her hair was like rubbed brass in the sunless twilight. "Just glad I'm not wearing high heels."

We were into a screening mass of tangled chamisa when Mike raised a warning hand. "Keep your heads down. We're coming up on something."

We arrived at the edge of a large clearing—and from our hiding place in the brush we saw Dibela's rusted-out truck parked behind a long, roughly constructed board shack.

"He's probably inside," said Mike, keeping his voice low. If there were any guards around, we didn't want to attract their attention.

At the farther side of the clearing was a second structure, much larger than the shack, raised from the ground on a platform of thick wooden stilts and made of what I guessed was thatched bamboo.

"Do you recognize that?" I asked Kelly. "Looks native to me."

"It is," she said softly. "A tribal ceremonial house . . . called a House of Skulls."

"Sounds cozy," I said. "Just the place for a family picnic."

"What kind of ceremonies go on in a joint like that?" asked Mike.

"Different kinds," Kelly replied, "but they all center around tribal magic."

"Something's sure going on in there right now," I said, as a rhythmic pulsing of drums began, backed by chanting voices. That's when we saw the door of the shack open and our boy Dibela emerge. Dressed just the way he was when he attacked me—a loincloth around his waist and his dark-bronze flesh daubed with colored paints. He had a bone through his nose, with a mass of feathers decorating his head. And he carried a spear.

"Holy shit!" breathed Mike.

"Dibela is more than a bartender," said Kelly. "He's also a tribal witch doctor."

We watched him cross the clearing and enter the House of Skulls. The chanting inside changed pitch, becoming more intense, almost frenzied.

Mike swung his head toward Kelly. "What would you guess they're up to?"

"Impossible to say from here."

"Then it looks like we go have ourselves a gander," Mike declared.

We scanned the area for guards. It looked safe. Guess they felt secure up here in the middle of nowhere. With Mike leading, we sprinted across the clearing, ducked between stilts, and crouched in the dry mustard grass beneath the House of Skulls.

Directly above, the platform shuddered under pounding feet—and the sound of the drums and chanting voices washed around us, a sea of alien sounds.

We crawled to a better vantage point. Through a wide opening in the platform we could see more than two dozen natives, wearing wigs of fiber and bark, and necklaces of teeth, their dark bodies decorated with shells and colored seeds.

Many of the dancers carried bamboo spears and bone daggers, their skin painted in bizarre patterns, feathers weaving as they swayed to the throbbing drums.

The interior walls were crowded with painted wooden shields and grotesquely carved tribal masks—and, of course, with skulls. Lots of skulls, with gaping, eyeless sockets and hanging jaws of yellowed bone. I figured a couple of them had been lopped off the bodies of Stomper Lee and Eddie Lansdale. God knew where the others came from.

Then I heard Mike draw in his breath sharply. "Jesus!" he whispered. "They've got a guy tied up in there!"

He was right. At the far end of the platform, on a makeshift altar, we could see their latest victim, a young man stripped to the waist with his hands and feet securely bound. His neck rested on a crude wooden block, and it was obvious they intended to behead him. *And* cut his heart out.

That's what this damn ceremony was all about. This was the "something special" Dibela left work early for. Another ritual murder.

"Here, take this," Mike said, handing his .38 to me. "I'm going to the car and call for some backup. We gotta stop this before it's too late."

"I'm no good with a gun," I protested. "You might need it if you run into trouble."

"I'll be okay," Mike declared. "If they begin the main action before I get back—the head and heart bit—then start shooting. They can't stand up against bullets with the weapons they have."

"And what happens when I run out of bullets?"

"Cops'll be here by then."

And he ducked away from us, running low across the clearing in the direction of the car.

Lucero didn't get far. Two big natives who were rounding the shack spotted him, and loosed their spears. One missed; the other didn't.

Mike was down with a bamboo spear through his right shoulder.

"Bastards!" I muttered, and brought up the gun. I was ready to fire when Kelly grabbed my arm.

"Don't!" she warned. "Save your bullets until they're really needed. If we reveal ourselves now, *nobody* has a chance."

"Okay . . . I guess that makes sense." I lowered the .38, sweating. The palms of my hands were slick and my jaw muscles ached. This case was no longer colorful; it had turned deadly and frightening. I was shaking with tension.

The two natives dragged Lucero to his feet, and one of them jerked the spear loose. Mike let out a cry of agony. The spear point had gone through the soft flesh of his upper shoulder, and there was a lot of blood coming from the wound. Plus a lot of pain. But he was not seriously hurt.

Not yet.

Kelly and I ducked back into the shadows beneath the platform as the two natives passed us, forcing Mike ahead of them into the House of Skulls.

Inside, a wave of hostile cries was directed at Mike. Dibela danced around him, shaking his spear, teeth bared like a hungry wolf.

Then another native emerged from the clearing. He hurried into the House of Skulls, spoke intently to Dibela. The witch doctor left for the shack, remained inside for a few moments, then returned to the ceremony.

"Something's going on at the shack," I said.

"What should we do?" Kelly faced me, her green eyes shaded with concern. "Should one of us try for the car?"

"No," I told her. "They'll be posting new guards now that Mike's been spotted. We have to stay right here."

Sure enough, just as I finished speaking, three painted natives, armed with spears, left the ceremonial house and began prowling around the clearing.

"I'm sure they won't think of looking under here," whispered Kelly. "We'll be safe for a while."

"Yeah," I muttered, gripping the .38 tightly in my right fist. "For a while."

"They're putting Mike on the altar with that other guy," Kelly pointed out. "That means—"

"I *know* what it means."

We watched and listened in shock as the drums began a faster beat; the dancing intensified, and the chanting mounted in volume. Things were heating up.

Dibela approached the altar. He'd replaced his spear with what was obviously a ceremonial blade. He waved it in the air, and the frenzied dancers let out a howl.

"Shit, he's gonna do it!" I told Kelly. "He's gonna lop off Mike's head!"

"Then I guess . . . it's time for you to start shooting," said Kelly.

My hand was shaking as I brought up the gun, aiming at Dibela through the gap in the flooring.

Now I had the .38 in both hands, trying to steady my aim, when that bronzed devil raised the blade full above him, ready to bring it down on Mike's neck. His eyes gleamed and a smile puckered his scarred face. The chanting was really crazed.

"Dave!" Mike yelled. "Shoot the sonuvabitch before he *kills* me!"

My finger was about to squeeze the trigger when three loud shots, like popping firecrackers, stunned the dancers into silence.

Dibela slowly turned from the altar, blood gouting from his head and chest. His glazed eyes were already dead as he dropped the blade and sprawled forward across the floor.

"It's Fraser-Shaw!" I gasped.

The rotund, white-suited consul general was standing in the doorway of the House of Skulls, a thin spiral of blue-gray smoke curling from the barrel of the big .45 automatic in his right hand.

Kelly and I lost no time in making our presence known. We scrambled from our hiding place and ran into the ceremonial house like two happy kids.

Fraser-Shaw had introduced himself and was cutting Mike and the other victim loose, with both of them babbling their thanks, when we arrived on the scene. The natives, utterly silent, had drawn back against the walls. I swung the .38 toward them, but they didn't seem to offer any threat. Their sick little show was over.

"Ah," said Fraser-Shaw, turning to face us. "Miss Rourke and Mr. Kincaid. I had no idea you were here."

"That goes double for us," I said. "Where did you come from? And how did you find this place? Are you alone?"

"Please." He raised a hand. "One question at a time, Mr. Kincaid. First, we must inquire as to the condition of these two gentlemen."

"I'm okay," said Mike. "Not much feeling in my right arm, but a lot of the bleeding's stopped."

Kelly was using her neck scarf as a makeshift bandage. I handed the .38 back to Lucero, glad to be rid of the damn thing.

"And what about you, young man?" Fraser-Shaw asked.

"I'm still . . . kinda . . . shook-up," he answered.

"That's quite understandable," said Fraser-Shaw. "However, let me assure you that there is nothing more to fear. Now that I have killed their witch doctor, these people are rendered powerless. Their magic has been lost."

"Who are you?" Kelly asked the young man.

"McCammon," he said. "Ben McCammon. I'm an assistant track coach at USC. These freaks kidnapped me from the athletic field last night. Man . . ." And he shook Fraser-Shaw's hand vigorously, "I'm just glad you showed when you did!"

"I'm going to call for backup," said Mike. "The rest of you stay here and keep an eye on these characters."

And Mike took off at a fast trot for the car.

Huddled close to the walls, the natives watched us silently.

Fraser-Shaw faced me. "Now, Mr. Kincaid, let me answer your questions. Your visit to my office yesterday roused my personal curiosity about the possible existence of a New Guinea cult in this area. I began an investigation and discovered that such a cult did indeed exist. The two recent murders were obviously the result of a brutal reversion to ancient tribal customs. Using my official status as a representative of Australia, I was able to locate one of these cultists. I found out he was going to attend some sort of ceremony."

"*This* ceremony?" I asked.

"Precisely," said the consul general. "I had no idea of its nature when I followed him here earlier today. Had I guessed it was another blood ritual, I would have brought along the authorities. I was, please understand, still operating from

43

theory. However, shortly after I arrived here, I was discovered. I was taken prisoner and tied up in the shack. Eventually I managed to free myself. I recovered the weapon I'd brought here with me, and was fortunate enough to intervene before more blood was spilled." He smiled at me. "It's as simple as that."

I stared at him. "You're a remarkable man, Sir Leslie. Really remarkable."

"Why, thank you."

"It's not a compliment," I told him—spinning abruptly on my left heel and karate-kicking the .45 from his hand. I scooped up the automatic and leveled it at his fat gut.

Kelly and McCammon were staring at me as if I'd gone round the bend.

"Dave!" Kelly protested. "What's *wrong* with you? He saved our lives!"

"He was just trying to save his own. Trying to keep himself out of jail—but he didn't quite make it. Did you, mate?"

Fraser-Shaw glared at me, eyes frosted, lips compressed. "When the police arrive, I'll have you arrested for assault," he said tightly.

"Sure you will," I said. And smiled.

Of course, there was no assault charge. Sir Leslie Fraser-Shaw was the one they arrested. For murder. When the shack was searched, no binding ropes or tape or handcuffs were found—but the sheriff's deputies *did* find the carved wood spirit mask and body robe worn by Sir Leslie when he participated in the blood ceremonies.

He'd come here to share McCammon's death, and was in the act of preparing himself for the ceremony when Mike's capture abruptly changed his plans. That's when he called Dibela to the shack and instructed him to proceed with the ceremony. Now that the cult's latest victim was a homicide cop, Fraser-Shaw realized things had gone too far. It was time to bail out. Dibela had been the only one who could identify the consul general; the others had seen him *only* in his masked role as a spirit of the dead. Therefore, with the death of the witch doctor, any evidence connecting Fraser-Shaw to the cult would vanish. So he decided to play "hero" and save Mike's life by shooting Dibela.

And it had almost worked.

"What I don't understand is how you knew the consul general was lying about being held captive," Kelly said.

"Noticed his wrist when he was holding the gun," I told her. "If he'd been bound and had struggled to free himself, the skin would have been chafed and raw. It wasn't. And that white summer suit of his—not a wrinkle or a smudge on it. So I knew he had to be lying."

Kelly shook her head. "I still can't figure why a man like Sir Leslie would involve himself in a blood cult."

"He was more than just involved," said Mike. "We got a full confession out of him. He was the guy behind the whole thing."

The three of us were in the Valley, sitting at a table at Jennifer's, another Aussie joint Kelly had discovered in Woodland Hills.

"That's right," I told her. "Fraser-Shaw began all this out of a sense of personal guilt. He felt the Aussies had mistreated the natives, including the ones in Papua New Guinea. Tribal cultures had been disrupted and destroyed. Then he found out about this core group from Papua. They'd immigrated to Los Angeles after independence. He began working with their leader, Renagi Dibela, to restore the ancient tribal customs. Even financed the building of the ceremonial house.

But the situation got out of hand with the reversion to cannibalism."

"Yet he went along with it?" Kelly asked.

"Yeah." Mike nodded. "The creep admitted to us that he actually began to *enjoy* that aspect of it. Gave him a real power lift. And damned if he didn't eat part of those missing hearts!"

"Oh, wow!" said Kelly with a grimace.

"Couldn't have tasted worse than Vegemite," I said.

She gave me a dirty look.

"Private joke," I told Mike.

Lucero stood up. "Well, I gotta split. Lots of paperwork waiting for me at the station." He looked down at Kelly and me. "Like I said before, you guys make a handsome couple!"

And, with a wide grin, he left the restaurant.

"Mike's an incurable romantic," I told Kelly. "Since my divorce, he's been trying to link me up with the right woman."

"I've got a great idea," said Kelly.

"What's that?"

"Let's go to your place and link up."

She was right. It *did* turn out to be a great idea.

The background here is quite real. In my manic sports car days, back in the 1950s and '60s, my friends and I used to stage tire-squealing night races over Mulholland Drive above the San Fernando Valley. Luckily, one could say miraculously, nobody was injured in these illegal events, and we all survived to become mature, safe-driving adults. But the memory of those insane runs is still clear and vivid. "Death Drag" was written with this dangerous activity in mind and dramatizes what could have happened up there on that wickedly-curving night road.

There are better ways to die.

Death Drag

It was one of those crazy-hot July nights and I was keyed-up and nervous and ready for something. Anything. I didn't much care. The clubroom was like a steam bath and I couldn't keep my mind on cards. I kept watching Maria. She was swaying and snapping her fingers to a lazy dance tune on the phono and once in a while she'd raise those eyes of hers and give me a look that said *C'mon over.* Finally, I'd had enough.

"I'm out," I said, pushing back my chair.

"Gonna call it a night, chum?" Herb asked me.

"Maybe," I said, stretching, "and maybe not." I didn't look at Stacey.

I walked over to the phono and flipped the needle off the disc. The music stopped—and so did Maria. She leaned back against the wall, a half-smile on her parted lips. She was eighteen and beautiful, with a hell of a fine figure, and she made what she had count. Her tight red dress emphasized the rising swell of her perfect breasts; her make-up was just right and she was always careful not to use too much. And she had a way of walking . . .

"Let's dance," I said, and I heard the card game stop behind me like somebody had announced the end of the world. I didn't need to turn around; I could feel the eyes on me, feel them all watching me—Herb and Angel and Stacey. Nobody moved.

"You—sure you wanna dance, Fred?" Maria asked me in that sexy voice of hers. She ran her pink tongue over her lips, her eyes steady on mine.

"I said so, didn't I?" Without turning, I slipped a fresh disc on the phono and snapped away my cigarette. "Let's go."

She came into my arms like she belonged there. This was the first time I'd held her, the first time any of us had the guts to cross Stacey, and I could tell by the way she smiled that Maria was pleased.

She was soft and warm and the music was great. But I knew it wouldn't last. And it didn't.

"Fred!" The one word, steely and hard and cold as ice, rang out in the room. We kept on dancing, but Maria was now tense in my arms; I could feel her quick breath on my cheek.

"Turn around, you bastard!"

We stopped dancing and Maria moved back. I turned to face Stacey Miller.

He was twenty-one, a year older than me, and he looked like a movie-star. I mean, handsome in a slick, hard kind of way. He was big—over six feet—and I'd seen what he could do with his hands. And he always carried a long, bone-handled knife . . .

He was smiling. "What made you do that, buddy boy?" His voice was as cold as his smile.

"Impulse," I snapped, my lips tight.

"Ya know," he said, moving toward me, "I think I'll fix it so you don't get any more *impulses*. Yeah—I think that's just what I'll do."

Herb and Angel melted off to one side of the room, leaving us in the center, like two boxers. I could see Maria by the table, watching us, excitement shining in her eyes.

"Look, I'm clean," I said, patting my pockets.

"So am I," said Stacey, and the bone-handled job clattered to the floor. "So what are we waiting for?"

His first blow caught me on the side of the head and spun me into the table. I covered up fast and came in low. We circled like two big cats. Stacey had the reach on me with those long arms of his, and I knew this wasn't going to be my night.

I found an opening and let him have a sharp right to the head, but he rolled with it and came back with one that cut my left cheek open. I could taste the salt blood on my lips.

I missed with another right and he closed in. Three quick hammer blows and I was on the floor, with Stacey on top of me, cutting my face up.

Then Maria stepped in.

"All right, Stace, back off. *Back off!*" She clawed at his neck, and he let me go finally. I heard that flat crack of his hand as he slapped her, but I couldn't do anything. I was still half-out.

"Don't you ever do that again, doll," he told her, his face red and twisted. "Understand?"

"Sure, Stace—but I only stopped you because I had a real crazy idea." She was breathing hard, one hand to her cheek. "I thought of—of something different."

"Name it," he said. "And it better be good."

"A drag," Maria gasped. "Over Mulholland Drive. Your Ford against Fred's Chevy."

"Yeah," nodded Stacey. "Yeah. That *would* be kicks. Well, what d'ya say, boy? You game for a little run?"

"As long as we get one thing straight," I said.

"And what's that?"

I looked up at him, wiping the blood from my lips. "Whoever wins the dice—wins Maria."

Stacey Miller smiled. "Okay, buddy boy. Now all you've got to do is *win*."

It was nearly one in the morning when we got to Sunset, and the boulevard was quiet as a cemetery. Whenever we jazzed our engines they sounded like machine guns.

Herb was with me in my Chevy and Maria rode with Stacey. Angel had stayed at the club.

"Think you can take him?" Herb asked me. He was a little guy, with a rat's pinched face and I didn't much like him. He got strictly nowhere with the dolls and I knew he liked to see a couple of guys go at each other over a chick like Maria.

"I can hang in a corner with that Ford," I said.

"I dunno." Herb shook his head. "His mill is hot, *real* hot."

Herb was right. Stacey knew how to soup a short all right. That Ford got up and stepped and no mistake. My Chevy was hot too, but it didn't have the juice to take Stacey on a straight. I was counting on the turns.

"Mulholland's a bitch at night," Herb said. "You know the road?"

"I been over it a couple of times in daylight."

"It's different at night, Fred. Take my word. The fog sticks to those hills like smoke. It's slick as hell up there and the turns come at you outa nowhere. Take my word."

"So what."

"So play it cool. Let Stace lead for awhile. Take him when he makes a mistake. It's always tougher to lead."

"Don't worry," I said, "I'll take him when I'm damn good and ready." I didn't want Herb's advice; he'd like to see us both get it and I was going to play this one by ear.

I knew how to handle the Chevy; I figured I could take Stacey. I thought of Maria in my arms—warm and curved and soft—and I wanted her. I wanted her bad.

Stacey raised an arm ahead of me. He was swinging into an all-night station and I followed him.

"Check your short," Stacey told me, opening the hood on the Ford. The service station guy was putting gas in his tank. "I don't believe in taking chances. Maria, honey, check the tires, willya? Make it 32 all the way round."

Stacey seemed plenty sure of himself and I began to wonder *why*. He didn't know how well I could corner the Chevy and there was no reason . . . And then I remembered! He used to live in North Hollywood, across the valley, before he moved out to Culver City. And that meant he'd taken Mulholland maybe a hundred times at night getting to the club, that he probably knew every curve and bump in the damn road.

Now I got the whole lousy setup. Maria had deliberately picked out this stretch because she was sure Stacey knew it, because she was sure he'd win and things would be settled once and for all. It wasn't enough seeing me cut up at the club; she wanted to see me go off of those hairpin turns up there. Well, it was too late to back down now. I'd just have to luck it through.

Maria was back beside Stacey inside the Ford, fixing her hair, ignoring me. I swore under my breath and climbed behind the wheel.

"Now listen, Fred," Stacey told me. "We'll follow Coldwater to Mulholland. Then we line up even and make our run to Laurel Canyon and back. Okay?"

I nodded and we were rolling again, taking it slow and easy up Coldwater because we didn't want to stir up any cops. They were like flies in Beverly Hills.

Herb didn't say anything all the way up; he knew I wasn't in any mood for talk.

We eased through the right-hand turn onto Mulholland and I pulled my Chevy up next to Stacey's Ford.

The road stretched away ahead of us, narrow and treacherous, with the fog riding it like a ghost.

Maria and Herb got out.

"We'll make one run," said Stacey. "Down to Laurel and back."

"Who'll count off for us?" I asked.

"I will," said Maria, and she stepped into the bright cone of our headlights. God, but she was beautiful! Despite myself, I wanted her now more than ever.

The match trembled in my hand as I lit a cigarette.

"Kinda shook, kid?" asked Stacey, running up the Ford's souped V-8. It sounded mean.

"Hell, no," I growled, stubbing out the cig and jazzing the Chevy's mill. "I'm cool."

I glanced once at the foggy length of night road and then focused my eyes on Maria, watching her upraised arm for the signal. I could see Herb's dark figure off to the left, like some kind of vulture, perched and waiting for the kill.

"Ready—set . . ."

I felt the sudden sweat on the palms of my hands and wished to hell I hadn't killed that cig. I needed it bad.

"Go!" Maria's arm flashed down.

We were off, engines at top revs, our tires squealing on the wet asphalt. I gave the Chevy all the pedal she'd take in first and held Stacey, but when I made my shift he was past me and moving for the first turn.

Stacey threw the Ford in—and I saw him fishtailing like mad. Something was haywire on the Ford; he was all over the damn road! I got through without much trouble.

The fog had thinned out in this section and I could see we had a bend ahead of us and then the road vanished. A cliff-edge hairpin curve!

Stacey was flat out. He was pushing the Ford for all it was worth. He ripped through a bend like a wild man, and then he was into the hairpin.

I knew he'd never make it.

The whole rear end of his car broke loose and slid sideways, and I could see him fighting the wheel. It didn't do any good. He was in the kind of slide that only ends one way.

If I live to be a thousand, I'll never be able to forget the nightmare roar he made, going down, slamming over rocks and brush and trees—clear to the bottom.

I stayed with Maria on the lip of the cliff while Herb climbed down to check on Stacey. We all knew what he'd find. Nobody lives through one like that.

I couldn't figure Maria. When I told her what had happened she didn't look surprised.

Then, suddenly, I realized *why* Stacey had gone over, what was wrong with his car. I could hear his voice, back there at the station, saying: *"Maria, honey, check the tires, willya?"* and I knew.

I looked down at her and she smiled, a beautiful, innocent smile, and I tipped her head back and kissed those sensuous lips, pulling her soft body hard against mine.

"I'm cold, Fred baby," she said, and her voice was silk. "C'mon, let's go back to the club."

"Yeah," I said, "let's go."

I often sit in all-night coffee shops listening to people talk. Sometimes I get lucky and end up with some great dialogue. Or a plot idea. Or the basis for an off-beat character.

My protagonist in this ironic crime tale is geared to react to what he overhears. His reaction tells my story.

The difference between me and Harper Riddick is that I don't follow people home from coffee shops, no matter what I hear them talk about. As a result, I'd never experience a night like this.

But who'd want to?

The Most Exciting Night of His Life

It was 3 a.m. and he was alone as usual. At the end of the counter. With half a cup of lukewarm coffee and an open paperback book in front of him. The new waitress, a faded blonde wearing too much mascara, asked him if he wanted a warmup. He said he did.

She took away his cup and brought him a fresh one, dark and steaming. No cream or sugar. Just straight black coffee. That's how he liked it.

"None of my business," the waitress said to him, "but I see you in here every night and I kinda wonder . . ."

"About what?"

"About what you do for a living. You got a day job?"

"I'm retired."

She gave a kind of grunt. "*You?* Naw, I don't buy it. You can't be over 30."

"I am. I'm 35."

"And you're *retired?*"

"Yeah."

"From what?"

"From my business."

"What kinda business?"

"Like you first said, it's none of *your* business about *my* business."

That shut her up. She drifted off to the other end of the counter to jabber with the fry cook.

He sipped his hot coffee.

His name was Harper Riddick and when he was in school they tried to call him "Harp." He didn't like it. Never got along with his classmates. Never dated, not even in high school. Girls were odd, unapproachable creatures who wanted you to spend money on them. Harper wouldn't do that.

He was lousy at sports, and his grade average was "C." When he dropped out of Taft High a year short of graduation his mother didn't say a word. She didn't care. His father had run off with a colored woman when Harper was five, so *he* didn't care either. His mother had some money from a family trust fund and she had supported Harper. Still did.

He had tried some jobs, but they didn't pan out. He usually got sore at his boss and told him to fuck off. Which got Harper fired. Finally he quit looking for jobs and just lived off his mother. She didn't give a damn. About him or what he did or didn't do. Had her own life. Always out whooping it up with a different boyfriend.

That's why Harper told people he was retired. Easy answer. What he liked to do best was to sleep all day then sit in all-night coffee shops like this one and read paperback thrillers. Mostly about hard-boiled detectives who smacked women around and drank a lot.

This waitress who'd asked him what he did was new on the counter. The other waitress, who used to serve him, knew enough to keep her mouth shut around him. Just pour his coffee and lay out his cherry pie a la mode and keep her trap zipped.

The new one would learn. She'd find out soon enough that he didn't like to gab with some stupid broad. Harper thought of all women as stupid broads. Like his mother. She was one.

He went back to his book, getting lost in it. He was into a good part where the gang had raped the detective's girl and was beating him up for trying to interfere. The detective was getting the crap beat out of him. Harper chuckled when one of the gang kicked the detective in the balls.

Which was when Harper began listening to the two men in the booth just left of the counter. They were talking in low voices, but Harper could hear everything they said. There was this tall one with bad teeth and long stringy hair and small rat's eyes, and there was the short one who was almost bald and had a big gut and a round moon face and sounded like a frog. He was saying . . .

". . . and I swear it's a really sweet setup. The old guy is alone at the house. Servants' night off. He'll be asleep upstairs. We pick the lock on the back door and go in that way. House alarm's been fixed."

"Suppose the old fart wakes up?" said the tall guy. "Suppose he's got a gun up there in his friggin' bedroom."

"He sleeps like a goddamn *log*. I know."

"How do you know?"

"He had a chauffeur that usta drive him around. Then he goes cheap and decides to drive himself, so the guy gets canned. Chauffeur told me about the whole layout, how it takes an earthquake to wake the old fart and where the safe is and how to open it. He even gave me the combination."

"No shit!" The bald guy whistled through his teeth. "So, is this chauffeur guy gonna be going inta the house with us?"

"Nix. It's just you an' me. We pay him his end after we fence the stuff. Keeps cash in there too. It's a real sweet haul."

"An' you wanta do it tonight?"

"Sure. It's like I said. Servants all off and him there alone. We'll go in, open the safe, grab the goodies and be out of there while he's still between snores."

Harper Riddick forgot all about his coffee and his paperback. He was trembling, and his upper lip was moist. He realized that these two men were about to commit a crime and that he, Harper, was now privy to their plans.

I could call the police, have them followed, and maybe collect a reward from their intended victim. Or . . . I could follow them and watch everything. Actually witness the crime!

The thought ran through his body like an electric shock. What an opportunity! To be on hand for a genuine break-and-enter. Not something out of one of his paperbacks, but the *real* thing.

To hell with the cops. Let them solve this, without his help. All cops are stupid. Why help out some stupid cops? Okay then, it was settled. When they left he'd follow. Share in the excitement.

Chance of a lifetime!

They had finished talking. Putting down money for the tip. Getting ready to go.

Hurriedly, Riddick drank the rest of his coffee and shoved the paperback into his pocket. He left a quarter on the counter, then ambled casually toward the cash register. They were already there, paying the bill. Harper came in behind them, laid out the exact change. The cashier nodded, and Riddick followed them outside to the asphalt parking lot. Sodium vapor lamps painted the lot a pale yellow, reminding Harper of curdled milk. The winter night was warm—typical L.A. weather.

The two men climbed into a high-wheeled black Ford truck with a new California license plate. The engine sounded smooth and powerful.

Harper slid behind the wheel of his mother's metallic-silver Plymouth Neon. She let him have it most of the time since her boyfriends had their own cars. The Neon was sleek and fast, but Harper had no interest in speed. He just wanted basic transportation, mostly from home to a coffee shop or once every month or so to the latest crime flick. He especially liked how Steven Seagal took the law into his own hands. *Way to go, Steven.*

The truck was heading east down the Ventura Freeway toward Hollywood. Maybe the rich guy owned a movie studio or something. Harper dreamed a lot about playing gangsters and mowing down stupid cops with a tommy gun. What a blast that would be!

They took the Highland Avenue turnoff past the Hollywood Bowl (all dark and silent at this time in the morning) and turned right on Sunset. Kept going—away from Hollywood, through the Sunset Strip, into Beverly Hills.

Harper kept at least five car lengths behind the Ford. Not a lot of traffic, so he didn't want to crowd too close. Keep them from being aware they were followed. Like in the paperbacks.

By the time they turned right off Sunset into Bel Air Riddick's heart was beating faster. *So this is where the rich guy's house is. A Bel Air mansion. The old fart must really be loaded. Safe probably chock full of cash and jewels.*

The black Ford stopped at the top of a rise overlooking a wide sweep of trees and blinking lights. Harper cut his engine and drifted to a stop in the night shadow of a big pepper tree.

He watched the two thieves exit the truck, look around to make sure they were alone, then move toward a tall glass-and-stone house. A black iron spike-topped fence surrounded the property.

Harper eased open the door of the Plymouth and got out, shutting it quietly behind him. He padded along the sidewalk toward the mansion, keeping to the wall shadows.

Each of the men carried a two-cell flashlight. He saw them use some kind of tool on the gate, causing it to swing open. They moved down the crushed-gravel drive to the rear of the house, to the kitchen entrance, where they used the same tool to open the door.

Now they were inside the mansion, leaving Harper alone in the darkness. *I've got to see it all,* he told himself. *I'm going in. Don't be a fool! It's too risky.*

I'm going inside.

And he entered the house through the open back door. Noises ahead of him. Coming from the den.

Where the safe was.

Harper crept forward until he reached the hall leading to the den. Breathing fast, he eased along it, keeping close to the wall. Reached the door.

They were silhouetted against the glow of their flashlights as Harper watched them open the safe.

"Good score," said the bald one.

"Yeah," said the tall guy. "You get the cash. I'll handle the jewelry."

They dumped everything into a canvas sack, shut the safe again and turned back for the hall.

Harper had already retreated to the foyer where he crouched in a patch of blackness under the main stairway. He expected them to leave by the kitchen, but they didn't.

They went upstairs.

Why? They *had* what they'd come for. Why go upstairs?

Harper moved out to peer up the wide stairway which curved away into darkness. A door opened. Then he heard a bumping, a curse, a shot (impossibly loud!) and the sound of a body thumping to the floor.

Jeez! They've killed the old man! Suddenly, nothing made any sense. *Why commit a murder when you have what you came for?*

They were returning to the lower floor now, carrying something between them: a large oil painting in a heavy gilt frame. What the hell was this? *No time. Have to leave. Get out ahead of them.*

Harper made his way down the hallway. To the kitchen. He had his hand on the knob of the outer door when a sharp blow to the back of his skull sent him spinning into blackness.

Harper Riddick awoke in the upstairs bedroom, next to a dead body. The old man, his mouth open, glazed eyes staring at nothing. At Riddick's feet: the bag of cash and jewels.

He sat up, dazed, blinking at the three men. Not two. *Three.* The bald one. The tall one. And a man in a dark suit with a long, cadaverous face and pale skin. Looked like an undertaker. Instinctively, Harper knew that this was the chauffeur—who had followed him as he followed the other two, who had waited in the kitchen to strike him down.

"Cops are on the way," said the bald one.

"Yeah, we just called 'em," said the tall man.

The chauffeur had a Colt Woodsman in his right hand. "This is the murder weapon," he said. "And the loot you took from the safe is all in that sack. You're a bad boy, Riddick!"

"How . . . how do you know who I am?"

"Oh, we know all about you," said the tall guy, grinning at him with those bad teeth. "Unmarried. No job. No girlfriend.

Live off your mother. Spend your nights in a coffee shop. A bum is what you are. A bum turned thief and killer."

"I didn't kill anybody!"

"That's not the way it's going down. After you forced the old man to give you the combo to the safe you shot him. Your prints are on the safe. We saw to that while you were beddy-bye."

"I don't understand," said Harper. His throat was tight, and it was difficult to speak. "Why are you doing this to me?"

"We needed someone to set up for tonight. We picked you," said the tall man.

"But you didn't need to kill anybody! You had what you came for—the money and the jewels."

The tall man shook his lean head slowly. "They're not what we came for."

"The painting . . . the one I saw you carry downstairs . . ."

"Yeah," nodded the bald man. "It's a genuine DeVega. Painted in 1513. Worth a fortune on the black market. Our dead friend here had it lifted from the Getty Museum last year. For his private collection. No one knows what happened to it. We walk away with it and the cops don't even know it was here."

"But why kill him to get it?" Harper asked numbly.

"He didn't give us any choice," said the tall man. "We couldn't just walk in and grab the painting. The old fart *knew* us."

"I told them about the DeVega," said the chauffeur. "We didn't figure on having to snuff him to get it. We figured he'd be reasonable."

"Right," nodded the bald man. "We offered him half the black market price if he'd let us fence the DeVega, but the stubborn bastard wouldn't go for it."

"Which meant he *had* to die," finished the chauffeur.

"Otherwise, when he found the painting gone he'd finger us for the job. Put out a contract on us."

"Which is where you fit in," added the tall man. "When the cops show up they'll find a dead thief with a bag of loot and the murder gun in his hand. Clean and simple."

Harper surged forward, but the chauffeur held his shoulder. "But I'm—"

"Alive," nodded the bald one. "You won't be when the cops get here."

"They'll know someone else shot me," protested Harper, bathed in sweat, his eyes darting from one face to the next.

"After you did the safe you came back here with the loot," said the chauffeur. "To make certain the old boy was dead. He wasn't. He lived just long enough to get his .45 from the night table and put a slug into you. He'll be holding the automatic. We'll put it in his hand. Then we put the Colt he died from in *your* hand. Clean and simple."

A rising sound of sirens in the distance.

"Time to split," said the bald man. "Thanks for helping us out, Harp."

And he pointed the shining .45 at Riddick's chest.

Just before the explosion that took his life, Harper Riddick could not help thinking, through the sweat and the terror, beyond the interior thunder of his beating heart, that, indeed, this had been the most exciting night of his life.

*I've always had the desire to write a Sherlock Holmes story, but was frustrated by the fact that literally dozens of other authors had written extensively about Holmes. Then I thought of a unique approach in which I could incorporate a new version of my favorite Holmes adventure, **The Hound of the Baskervilles,** into a story about the Great Detective.*

*Ah, what a challenge—to bring that legendary slavering beast-dog to Mars and involve my ultra-tough private eye, Sam Space, in the caper. (I was fortunate enough to win an Edgar Allan Poe Special Award in 1972 for my initial novel about Sam, **Space for Hire,** and I followed up with a sequel novel and four shorter Space tales.)*

I cannot imagine how any writer could have more fun than I did in bringing Holmes and Watson to the Red Planet. Writing "The Beast of Bubble City" was a truly joyful experience.

Solve the mystery.

Meet the Beast.

The Beast of Bubble City

I have never been a man given to petty complaints, but the inclement weather conditions in Bubble City on this particular morning had put me into something approaching a severe snit. Curtains of gritty red sand whirled and gusted around me as I exited the hoverkab. Unsnapping my nearleather coinpurse, I consulted the glowcard which told me the fare was an even ten solarcredits. I carefully counted out the required ten, added two more as a tip, and slipped the coins into the tummyslot of the gum-chewing robo kabbie.

"You call *that* a tip?" he growled. "This is the Christmas season, bud. How much Christmas cheer can I buy with two lousy solarcreds?"

"I am well aware of the season," I told him. "And it seems to me, my dear fellow, that two solarcredits is an ample reward for your services in delivering me to this address. I shall not be badgered into giving you more."

"Up yours," snarled the kabbie, climbing back into his egg-shaped machine and whisking off through the sand.

Ungrateful clod! I gripped my cane in anger. Was it not enough that I had been forced to leave the comfortable lodgings at 221B to venture out on such a foul day upon the urgent request of my friend Sherlock Holmes? Must I also endure being insulted by a rude vulgarian? Indeed, the morning was ill begun.

I shook sand from my cape and adjusted my bowler as I approached the offices of the man I had been dispatched to find. The hallway of the building reeked of boiled cabbage, which I found indeed peculiar. Was cooking allowed in a commercial business establishment? Well, this was a most unsavoury section of town, and I supposed that the strictures of more civilised society did not apply here.

Ah, the correct door, proclaiming, in sputtering, begrimed neon letters:

SAMUEL T. SPACE
Investigations

On Earth, Mr. Space would be referred to as a 'private orb'. An entire body of cheap literature had burgeoned around such individuals, replete with punchouts, explosions of hand weaponry, violent pursuits, and rapid exchanges of lurid street argot. One would hope that here on Mars such excesses might be greatly modified.

I opened the door and entered, expecting to encounter the usual secretary. Not so. The waiting room was unoccupied, although a desk and empty chair confronted me. At that moment the door to the inner office was opened by Mr. Space himself. His timeworn zipcoat, rumpled trousers and scuffed brown shoes told me I had the right man. Holmes had described his unwholesome attire in some detail.

"Hello, pal," said the shoddy detective. "You'll have to excuse the fact that my robo secretary isn't here to buzz you in. Had to send her back to the shop to have her buttocks refurbished. Edna's a good kid. Keeps the bill collectors off my back—of which you're not one, eh?"

"No, I am most assuredly not."

"I could tell from your fancy duds." He stood aside and gestured me to a chipped nearchair. Then he settled into place behind an unsightly desk whose glowtubing had shorted out. I noted a brown fedora with a turn-down brim under a bell-jar on the desk, marked 'Classic Hat'. How colorfully eccentric!

"So . . . let's open your can of beans."

"I am not carrying foodstuffs on my person," I informed him.

"I meant . . . what's on your mind, fella? Just who are you?"

"John H. Watson, M.D.," I replied, presenting my card. "I came directly from the Hu Albin Amazing Automated Crime Clinic at Red Sands Avenue and 72nd Street here in Bubble City. I reside with my friend Mr. Sherlock Holmes in an upper flat at 221B."

"Sure, I know Albin's joint. Me and ole Hu go way back. He's been renting out those robo detectives of his since I was in knee pants. Last time I saw him he'd just added Bulldog Drummond and Miss Marple to his string. Already had Philo

Vance, Boston Blackie, Charlie Chan and Nero Wolfe. Plus your pal, Sherlock. Who was a little wacko the day I was there."

"Holmes . . . 'wacko' . . . Surely you jest."

"Nope, I'm feeding you the straight goods. Sherlock must have had a couple of screws loose because he pulled a horse pistol on me and insisted I was the infamous Professor Moriarty. Might have damn well shot me if Albin hadn't conked him with a champagne bottle. Hu apologized for the problem. Told me Holmes would be hunky-dory once he had his solenoids replaced."

"Mr. Holmes is perfectly sound now, I assure you."

"That's good to hear. So . . . what brought you to my neck of the woods?"

"My conveyance was an egg-shaped hoverkab."

"Don't take everything I say so damned literally," Space protested, plainly vexed. "Just tell me what you want."

"Mr. Holmes insisted that I come here straight away to fetch you. He is most anxious to be rented."

Space made an unpleasant snorting sound. "Forget it! The last time I rented one of Hu's robos, the damn machine squashed my mechanised cat."

I bristled at his words. "Sherlock Holmes is much more than a 'damn machine', Mr. Space. He possesses the most brilliant, supremely deductive mind in the entire solar system."

"Yeah, well maybe he does—when his wires aren't crossed. But why should I rent him? I don't need extra help. My caseload is anything but fat right now."

"You fail to understand the situation, sir," I declared. "Being a robot under the ownership of Mr. Hubert Albin, my friend is not a free agent. He cannot rent himself. In order for him to work on a case he must be acquired by a legally qualified second party. You, Mr. Space, are that second party."

"You mean, he needs *me* to bail him out so he can go solve some case that's bugging him?"

"Precisely!" I nodded. "It has come to Holmes's attention that his services are urgently required at Baskerville Hall. The family curse is once again exacting its fearful toll. Two of the male Baskervilles, in the direct line of descent, have, on the moor within these past months, been mauled and savaged in a most appalling manner." My voice rose with the heat of emotion. "Only Sherlock Holmes can save the final heir to the Baskerville fortune. Even as we speak the life of young Jonathan Baskerville hangs in the balance." I stood up from the chair, waving my cane. "I tell you, sir, the Hound of the Baskervilles once again stalks Grimpen Moor!"

Space was grinning at me. "That's some speech, Doc. You remind me of a guy I worked for once on a Neptunian pig caper. Talked just the way you do. Lots of bluster and bombast. Even had a dinky little moustache like yours. He hired me to find out who was stealing all of his prize pigs from this farm he owned on Neptune. I disguised myself as a fat porker and rooted around in the pigpen—a nasty job, I can tell you—until these two pignappers showed up. Real mean characters. Frogboys from the Luani cluster. They have these super-long green tongues they catch bugs with and I—"

"Please, Mr. Space, must you regale me with useless flummery from your past? I am here upon a vital mission regarding the House of Baskerville. There is simply no time for this pig twaddle!"

"Fine," he said. "You want to talk about the Baskervilles? I know all about 'em. Rich as sin. When they emigrated to Bubble City last year they had the family castle dismantled and shipped up here in a special rocket. Even imported their own moor. And, from what you've told me, they also brought along the family curse."

"Indeed they did!" I declared.

Another unpleasant snort from the seedy detective. "Tommyrot! There *is* no curse and never was. The Hound is pure flapdoodle, a fairy tale made up to scare witless idiots. I read about these two murders—and it's obvious that somebody is after the family. An old enemy maybe. Or a psycho who just hates their guts. I don't know who killed those poor schmucks out on that moor, but you can bet it sure wasn't any hound from Hell."

"You are a rigid, cynical man, Mr. Space."

"No, I'm a realist. I just don't happen to believe in fairy tales."

I sighed. "Believe what you must, but your intransigence has no bearing on the reason for my visit here. Will you, sir, in the name of justice, rent Mr. Sherlock Holmes so that he may be permitted to save the life of Jonathan Baskerville?"

"Why me? Why can't the Baskervilles go rent your tin pal on their own?"

"Because they are not qualified to do so. A robot detective can be retained only by an officer of the law, a court official, or a licensed private investigator. Those are the rules."

"Okey doke, let's say I agree to play in your ballpark. What's in it for me? I'm gonna need some heavy scratch."

"That poses no problem. As you know, the Baskervilles are extremely well endowed financially. Holmes will see to it that you are reimbursed his rental fee and paid a very handsome sum for your cooperation in this matter."

"*How* handsome?"

"He has named a figure of five thousand solarcredits."

The rumpled detective stood up. "Doc . . . you got yourself a deal." He lifted the bell-jar to remove his classic hat, clapped it on his head, and accompanied me from the office.

The game, as my learned friend so often remarked, was truly afoot.

★ ★ ★ ★ ★

Mr. Hubert Albin met us at the Crime Clinic and seemed genuinely pleased to encounter the grubby detective once again.

"Hey, Sam! Long time no see!" Albin pumped his friend's hand in a vigorous manner.

"Yeah, it's been a while."

"You know, the other day I got to thinking about that pig guy from Neptune—the one who stiffed you out of your fee after you played porker for him in order to grab those two froggies."

Space nodded. "The creep really did a number on me. I had to pawn my electronic chimp to pay the office rent." He shook his head sadly. "I really loved that monkey."

"Whatever happened to him?"

"The chimp?"

"No, the pig guy."

"Well now, that's quite a story," began Space.

"Come, come, gentlemen!" I protested. "We are here to see Sherlock Holmes. Cannot these porcine recollections be explored at another more propitious time?"

Albin shot a smile at Space. "So the good doc convinced you to rent out ole Sherlock, eh?"

"You got it, Hu. That's why I'm here."

As we rode a jumplift to the upper level, Space asked how things were going at the clinic.

"Well, crime is always good during the Christmas season," said Albin, "so I've been renting out some of the robos, but it's tough trying to keep them in shape. Miss Marple is always yapping about her chilblains and Philo Vance keeps wetting his bed. Then, last week, Travis McGee ran off to Florida with the robot maid."

"Is Holmes functioning okay?" inquired Space. "I don't

69

want any more horse pistols pointed at me."

"He's in great shape. Just finished rewiring his cortex."

Albin opened the door to 221B and the rumpled detective whistled through his teeth. "Wow! You've really done a job here!"

Hu Albin nodded proudly. "Cost me a bundle, lemme tellya. It's an exact duplicate of the original London sitting room from Baker Street."

He pointed out the bearskin rug and elephant's-foot umbrella stand, the deep armchair by the fireplace, the Persian slipper holding Sherlock's tobacco, the tall bookcase jammed with technical tomes and journals, the collection of antique pipes on the desk, and the research area in the corner, fully stocked with chemicals and scientific paraphernalia. Two alabaster lamps were reflected in the wide mirror above the mantel, and a crystal decanter of Napoleon brandy stood on the Indian coffee table.

I felt a warm glow suffuse me; I was very fond of this room.

"You've done yourself proud, Hu," Space declared. "But where's Sherlock?"

"In the sound-proof closet," said Albin. "I can't stand listening to him sawing away on his damn fiddle."

"Yeah," nodded Space. "That kind of noise can drive you bats. Now, if he played a good jazz trumpet . . ."

Albin opened the closet door. "Hey, Sherl, you got company."

It was odious to hear Holmes referred to as 'Sherl', but the great man took it in his stride, smiling thinly and setting aside his violin. He extended a lean-fingered hand to the grinning detective.

"Ah, Mr. Space, we meet again. I trust you have forgiven my somewhat aberrant behavior when last you graced these humble lodgings."

"Sure, sure. No sweat."

Holmes broadened his smile. "I am duly gratified to know that Dr. Watson was able to prevail upon your good nature in having you come here at such short notice."

"My good nature had nothing to do with it," Space corrected him. "It's the dough I'm after."

"Ah, but of course. Personal remuneration is always a primary factor. I assume the good doctor named the amount I am prepared to have paid to you through the Baskerville auspices?"

"Yep. Five thou—plus what I'll be shelling out to rent you."

"Then we are in mutual accord?"

"Definitely."

Holmes withdrew his caped greatcoat and deerstalker from the clothes rack. "We must make haste, Watson. Time is of the essence if I am to intervene in this dark business and save the last male Baskerville from a grisly and distressing death upon Grimpen Moor."

Albin had already prepared the necessary rental forms, and once Mr. Space had affixed his signature and turned over the proper sum of money the transaction was complete. The great man was free to go.

"You may return to your unkempt offices, Mr. Space, while Watson and I pursue this most urgent affair," Holmes told him. "I shall, of course, see to it, my dear chap, that the agreed-upon sum is delivered to you upon my—"

"No dice, Sherlock!" Space cut in rudely. "I'm sticking with you for the whole nine yards. If your skull gets ripped off out on that moor I don't get my fee, plus I lose my deposit, plus I have to pay for your new head. So, my 'dear chap,' we're together on this one all the way, whether you like it or not."

"Very well," nodded Holmes. "So long as I am allowed to

handle the case exactly as I see fit, without interference of any sort. Is this understood?"

"Yeah," said Space. "The caper's all yours."

"Then let us repair at once to Baskerville Hall." He turned to me. "Watson, would you be so kind as to summon a kab?"

As I left to do so I heard Mr. Albin chuckle: "Good luck, Sam. I hope you and Sherlock come back in one piece."

It was a sentiment I wholeheartedly endorsed.

Baskerville Hall was at the fringe of Bubble City, part of the new Martian Urbanization Development Project sponsored by the mayor and city council. The Baskervilles had been given a large amount of tax-free land in return for their emigration to the Red Planet. As the richest family in Bubble City, they had brought prestige to the area. At least until the curse became public knowledge with the shocking deaths of Alexander and Reginald Baskerville. Now the family name was associated with madness and murder.

The house itself was massive, sprawling across a full acre, a castle-like assemblage of stone and wood and glass and brick, of crenellated towers, of turrets and battlements and courtyards and formal gardens.

Jonathan's aunt, Dame Agatha, a stout, rosy-cheeked woman in her mid-sixties who had initially phoned Holmes at the Crime Clinic, took us on a tour of the house. Holmes displayed particular interest in the library, with its vaulted Tudor ceiling and gracefully arched doorway, carefully examining several of the richly bound volumes contained therein.

Eventually, we were led to the west wing in which resided Sir Jonathan Rodney Baskerville, the last heir to the vast family estate. The lad was unmarried and there were no other children to carry on the Baskerville name.

Sir Jonathan awaited us in his ornate bedroom fitted out like a king's chambers. He was propped up with pillows in a high-backed gilt antique chair next to a crackling hearth fire. He gave each of us his bony, cold-fleshed hand to shake, seemed exhausted by the effort, and fell back into the pillows with a groan of pure anguish.

"Jonathan is terrified of the Beast," Dame Agatha informed us. "He is certain it will find a way to strike him down—although he seldom ventures beyond the confines of these four walls."

The youth was fearfully unattractive. Small of stature, with bird-thin legs, frail arms, and a long reedy neck, his undersized head sat above his sloped shoulders like an egg on a stick. Although still in his early twenties, he was almost completely bald; a thin mist of hair did little to conceal the high dome of his forehead, and his eyes were pale and watery above a beaked nose and a thin, nearly lipless mouth. In all, a most unprepossessing individual.

After greeting the young heir, Holmes said very little, but had been poking about the room; now he walked to the high leaded windows, drawing back the thick brocade curtains. Below, spreading over a wide area, like a befouled grey blanket, lay Grimpen Moor. It was late afternoon and ominous black granite outcroppings threw long, jagged shadows across the moor's barren surface. It was a sere, desolate landscape of bracken and bramble, of dripping moss, of stunted trees with gnarled roots, of lichen and gorse, green-scummed ponds, deep bog holes and cragged cairns.

"I beseech you, close the curtains!" Jonathan croaked. "I cannot bear that awful view. It oppresses me mightily."

"Why then, Sir Jonathan, remain in a room which overlooks the moor?" queried Holmes. "You could easily occupy other quarters."

Young Baskerville shook his balding head. "No, no. I must face my enemy. The Hound is out there, and I cannot deny its foul presence."

"Have you actually *seen* this creature?" I asked him.

"Yes! On two occasions—the nights my brothers met their fate. My first sighting of the Beast was when I was watching Alex cross the moor from my windows. Suddenly, as if from nowhere, an immense hound, bathed in spectral fire with phospor-red eyes, leapt from a stand of boulders and struck out after my brother. It moved over the terrain with frightening speed. Alex heard it coming, and turned to face it, hands thrown protectively across his face. The creature sprang forward and . . . and . . ."

Baskerville closed his eyes against the dreadful image, lapsing into sobs, his body quivering with the horror of remembrance.

"And you witnessed Reginald's death in the same manner the following month?" asked Holmes.

"Yes! . . . God help me, yes."

"And is it not true, Sir Jonathan, that on both of these fated nights, the twin moons of Mars were at the full?"

"Yes. On both nights. That's why I could see so clearly what was happening out there on the moor. I witnessed both murders from this very room!"

"Seems to me you could have opened the damn window and yelled a warning," said Space, now directly facing Baskerville. "When you saw that thing go after them, why didn't you yell?"

"I was frozen with fear," said the pale young man. "My throat was locked tight. And even if I *had* shouted a warning, what possible good would it have done? My brothers were doomed from the moment they set foot on Grimpen Moor."

I posed a basic question. "After Alexander's grisly death,

why did Sir Reginald choose to traverse the moor after dark?"

"Reggie was a stubborn fool who mistakenly believed that he could defeat the creature who had struck down Alex. I did my best to warn him of the family curse, but he scoffed at the idea, and coldly ignored my fervent pleas not to walk Grimpen Moor once the sun had set."

"Was Sir Reginald armed at the time of his encounter?" asked Holmes. "The newspapers indicated that two weapons were found near the body."

"That's correct," said the youth. "Reggie carried a brace of fully loaded pistols with him that night. During the attack, I saw him fire point-blank at the Beast, unleashing a veritable hail of bullets, but they had absolutely no effect. I tell you, Mr. Holmes, this creature is not of mortal flesh, it is of the Devil himself!"

Holmes folded his arms behind his back, a glint of determination in his shadowed eyes. I had seen him like this many times and I knew he was about to do something extraordinary.

"I intend to explore the moor tonight," he told us. "Both moons will again be at the full and conditions should be ideal."

I was incredulous. "Ideal? Ideal for *what*, in heaven's name? For the Hellhound's attack? Great Scott, Holmes, are you bent on achieving your own destruction at the jaws of this horror?"

"Not at all, my dear Watson," he told me, a casual note to his tone. "I have already formed a theory about the Hound, and I assure you I shall be in no great jeopardy if I am correct."

"And what if you are *not* correct?"

Holmes smiled indulgently, tenting his long-fingered hands. "When have I ever been wrong in matters of deduction?"

"What the doc here is saying makes a lot of sense to me," argued Space. "If you insist on going out on that lousy moor tonight I'll have to go with you to protect my investment. And lemme tellya, it's the last frigging place I want to be!"

"Tush, my dear fellow," said Holmes. "Your highly emotional concern is wholly unfounded. I am sure no one will be at risk. Are you also planning to attend me, Watson?"

I nodded gravely. "I shall be at your side whatever the cost. Although, in my view, such action is utter madness."

Jonathan was leaning forward, his eyes wild. A frail hand gripped Holmes at the elbow. "I beg of you, sir, as I beg of your two companions . . . do not set foot on Grimpen Moor this night! The Hound is out there, and he will most surely attack. Any weapons you might carry will be of no avail since, I swear to you, nothing can stop him. *Nothing!*"

Holmes gently extracted his arm from young Baskerville's bony fingers and moved to the door. "I intend to indulge in a light repast, taken in my rooms, followed by a bit of reading in the library. Whereupon I shall nap until it is time for us to meet at the edge of Grimpen Moor."

And he exited the bedroom, leaving us to stare in numbed shock at one another.

I knew enough about Sherlock Holmes to recognize his desire to ponder the case at hand, and I was careful not to disturb him, or in any way intrude upon his privacy, for the remainder of that long evening. After dinner, which I had served to me in the south wing, and to help calm my mounting sense of apprehension, I engaged in several spirited games of chess with Mr. Space. His being able to play was something of a pleasant surprise, since I had not expected a person of his lower station to have mastered such a game. And master it he had, wresting victory from me three times out of five. In my own defence, however, I must point out that I was not myself, in terms of mental agility, with half my mind mulling over the dangers inherent in our imminent rendezvous with the spectral Beast.

During the course of these games, Mr. Space expressed serious concern over the operation Hu Albin had performed on Holmes's cortex. Indeed, *had* my robot friend been properly wired? Perhaps not, given his 'nutso plan' (as Mr. Space put it) to walk us straight into the jaws of doom.

And thus the hours passed . . .

Now we stood in the pitch of deep night at the dank edge of Grimpen Moor: Holmes, myself, and Samuel Space. A moaning wind had risen, increasing our discomfort, and the broken terrain stretching ahead seemed to promise unseen horrors.

It was reported to us by Dame Agatha that Jonathan was so distraught over our foolhardy expedition that he had locked himself inside his chambers and taken to bed. She herself was equally upset at the prospect of our journey, cautioning us in particular to watch out for quagmires and treacherous bog holes.

How clearly I recall the good woman's strained features as she delivered her dire warning: "The moor can suck an entire horse and wagon under in less than a minute. I've seen it happen with my own eyes, and a most harrowing sight it is! Always keep to the solid paths, on firm ground, lest you be sucked into the bog. I pray you, hark well to my words!"

Thus, we had a troublesome new worry to add to the threat of the Hound itself. Holmes was, as always, imperturbable and staunchly resolute. Standing at his side by the moor's edge afforded me a modicum of courage on this night when courage was sorely needed.

Reaching into his greatcoat to consult his gold pocket watch, Holmes nodded to us. "Time to embark, gentlemen.

Onward! The game's afoot!"

We struck off on a narrow path over the great moor. Above us, the twin moons of Mars illumined the bowl of night sky. Carried by the wind, the miasmic odour of slimed plant life, rotting ferns and scummed ponds permeated my nostrils, a mephitic stench of mould and decay indigenous to such a foul arena.

Despite Sir Jonathan's protestations that weaponry would be useless, we were well armed. I had a loaded pistol within instant reach and Space carried a lethal .45-calibre Earth automatic in a shoulder holster. Holmes, too, was 'packing heat' (as Sam so colorfully phrased it). He had a Webley service revolver belted beneath his outer attire.

Surely no animal, however fierce, could stand against such potent firepower—yet the disquieting words of Sir Jonathan kept rising to the surface of my mind: "I tell you . . . this creature is not of mortal flesh, it is of the Devil himself!"

We were a good mile into our journey, following a succession of grassy paths that zigzagged through the moor, and had just passed a high bank of mossed black granite when a truly blood-chilling howl split the night, a sound of such incredible menace that it stopped us full in our tracks.

The cry of the Hound!

"Ah," said Holmes, scanning the sweep of moor with narrowed eyes, "I see that our monstrous friend is indeed in the vicinity, just as I surmised he would be. I wager he will be paying us a personal visit in very short order."

He spoke in a faintly musing tone, demonstrating no sign of the panic welling within me. Space, too, looked ashen in the silvered light of the double moons. We both had our guns out as we peered apprehensively into the shrouding gloom. Where was the Beast? How close?

"Come, gentlemen," said Holmes. "Let us proceed, but

with a maximum of caution, maintaining a sharp watch for our redoubtable adversary."

As we moved forward again, I kept darting my head around, striving to make out the phantom shape that stalked us. Jonathan was correct; only a fool would willingly venture here under such horrific conditions. At that fateful moment, in the wind-swept darkness of the moor, I could not help but believe the three of us fools. Perhaps Holmes's wiring had gone awry. It would explain his seemingly bland disregard for our personal safety.

Then . . . another blood-freezing howl, much closer.

It was coming for us now, and I could hear the drumming sound of its gigantic paws on the path behind us. Thump . . . thump . . . thump . . . Closer.

Very close now.

I had swung around, my eyes starting from my head in fear, a blade of ice running up my spine. I raised my pistol, cocking it. Space swore under his breath, clutching the big .45 in both hands.

"Yes," said Holmes, turning to face our onrushing enemy, "it is time for weapons—although do not expect your bullets to deter this creature."

"My God, Holmes!" I cried. "You've brought us all out here to die!"

Holmes gripped my shoulder. "Steady, Watson, steady!"

"You damn crazy robo!" shouted Space. "We don't have a chance in hell against this thing."

"Not in hell, perhaps," replied Holmes, his service revolver poised, "but here, on Grimpen Moor, the situation is quite different. Heads up, gentlemen, for the Beast is upon us!"

And then we saw it—loping rapidly toward us, snarling, with fanged teeth, covered with a bristling coat of ragged fur.

Its eyes burned with an unholy fire in the moon-shafted night.

Space and I fired simultaneously, hitting our target full on, but our rounds passed through the charging monster like water through a sieve. All was lost; we were facing sure and certain extinction.

Then, with the slavering creature only scant feet away, Holmes brought up his revolver and fired a single shot. The giant howled in pain, falling back, slipping from the path into the sucking mire. Instantly, it began to sink as life ebbed from its body.

"Quick, Watson!" shouted Holmes. "Help me free it. We cannot allow it to be lost!"

"But . . . but *why not?*" I sputtered. "Isn't this what we came for?"

"Don't argue the point, man! Just *help* me!"

Sam also pitched in; working together, the three of us managed to drag the bog-slimed monster back to firm ground.

As I was later to realize, Holmes had precisely timed our adventure. A faint skein of light was beginning to stain the edge of the Martian sky. The sun would soon be above the horizon.

I stared down at our fearsome enemy. The animal was quite obviously dead, its fanged mouth hideously agape, its eyes wide and unblinking. A froth of crimson seeped from its open jaw and the rank fur covering its chest was matted with blood. Holmes's shot had proven fatal.

"That's sure one ugly-looking critter," declared Space. He turned to my friend, a perplexed frown creasing his features. "How could you be so certain of killing it? And with just one shot. Our bullets didn't *faze* the damn thing. There's a lot about this I don't understand."

And then Sherlock Holmes explained the mystery . . .

"The first suspicious element I noted, within the scope of our conversation with Sir Jonathan at Baskerville Hall, was the degree of inner hostility he harbored for his two deceased siblings. I sensed his contempt for Alexander, and you will recall that he dubbed Sir Reginald a 'stubborn fool'. He showed no remorse whatever over their violent passing. What emotion he *did* display was sham."

Holmes had always possessed an uncanny ability to probe beneath the surface of one's personality, to root out hidden truths in us all. Now he continued:

"You will, I am certain, also recall my curiosity as to why Sir Jonathan would wish to occupy chambers featuring a direct view of the area he pretended to fear and loathe. Why should he remain in a room facing the moor when he could so easily have availed himself of other quarters? When I questioned him, he gave no satisfactory answer. The truth is, gentlemen, the moor was his killing ground and he was out *here,* in this very area, on the two nights his brothers were so savagely butchered."

"But Holmes," I protested, "Jonathan's aunt told me, upon hearing cries of despair from the moor on both of those fateful nights, that she had rushed upstairs and locked his door from the outside to protect him from possible harm. She had the *only* key. When she unlocked the door to check on him later, he was in the bedroom with his horror story of what he had seen through the window. This happened on both occasions. Thus, if he were out here on the moor at the time of the murders, as you claim he was, how could he have left his room, let alone later re-entered it, having no key of his own?"

"Elementary, my dear chap," said Holmes. "While I was pottering about in Sir Jonathan's bedroom I came upon a small clod of hardened dirt wedged between the rug and the edge of the wall. From the distinctive color and texture of the clod I ascertained that it had come from Grimpen Moor. I then discovered a hidden door, behind the closed drapery and set flush with the wall and extremely difficult to detect. I didn't have to open the door to know that the stairs behind it led directly down to the moor. Which is why Jonathan chose this particular room for his bedchamber. The clod of earth had dropped, unnoticed, from his shoe as he returned to the room after one of his nefarious excursions."

"Amazing!" I whispered, in genuine awe of the man. "Absolutely amazing."

"Finally," Holmes continued, "I noted several volumes in the library dealing with the occult, each of them bearing the personal bookplate of Jonathan Rodney Baskerville. The lore in these books pertained directly to the twin Martian moons."

"In what way?" asked Space.

"The fact that the moons were full on the night of each murder told me that our Hound was no ordinary animal. Under a full moon, certain tainted individuals revert to a primitive animalistic state. Their bodies attain great strength and agility—as we have witnessed in the case at hand."

I stared down at the corpse. The wind had ceased and the sun was just edging the dun-coloured expanse of moor. "Are you telling us," I asked, "that Sir Jonathan was *himself* the Hound of the Baskervilles?"

"Not a hound, Watson, but a wolf," said Holmes. "To be wholly accurate, a *were*wolf."

Under the sun's rays, the features of the Beast began to shift and change. The matted fur seemed to melt back into the body; the fanged jaw became a thin-lipped mouth; the ferocious eyes softened, becoming the eyes of . . .

"Sir Jonathan!" Space said in a shocked tone.

"We couldn't kill him!" I said to Holmes. "Our shots were totally ineffective. How could *you* have—"

"I used one of these," said Holmes, freeing a round from his service revolver. He held it up and the cartridge glittered brightly. "A silver bullet," he said. "The only sure way to kill a werewolf."

"You mean, you brought silver bullets *with* you?" asked Space.

"I never discount any form of superstition," said the great detective. "And while I had not previously encountered a werewolf, I nevertheless took the precaution of keeping several silver bullets among my stock of ammunition. When I noted the fact, in news accounts, that there were full moons on the nights of each murder, I therefore decided it would be prudent to take these special rounds with me to Baskerville Hall."

"Then Sir Jonathan's life was never in danger," I stated. "He killed his two brothers in order to inherit the family fortune. The curse regarding the spectral Hound of the Baskervilles was a hoax."

"Not entirely," said Holmes. "Remember, Watson, there *was* a curse involved here—the dark curse of lycanthropy."

I looked down at the slight pale body lying motionless in the early morning light. And I shuddered. Man into wolf, and now wolf into man.

The complex marvels of our universe can never truly be fathomed.

A final notation on this bizarre affair . . .

Of late, in the aftermath of our incredible adventure on Grimpen Moor, I find myself gripped with the unsettling conviction that my dear friend and companion, Mr. Sherlock Holmes, is—in reality—the infamous master of crime, Professor Moriarty.

However, Hu Albin has assured me that I will be one hundred per cent 'hunky dory' again once my solenoids have been replaced. He will perform the operation on Christmas Day.

Which, for a troubled robot, will be a fine and welcome Yuletide gift.

The Depression years spawned a bold new breed of des-
perado: Dillinger . . . Pretty Boy Floyd . . . Ma Barker . . .
Baby Face Nelson . . . Bonnie and Clyde. In the public eye,
these road bandits and bank robbers became almost heroic
as they defied the law, made daily headlines, battled au-
thority, and carved their own bullet-riddled niche in Amer-
ican culture.

My amoral young 1930s protagonist of "A Good Day"
reflects the influence of these larger-than-life lawbreakers.
For him, they are role models; their violent way of life is
darkly attractive.

Hal, of "A Good Day," is very much a product of his
time, dangerous, degenerate, and utterly cold-blooded.

And he's certainly no hero.

A Good Day

I shot him in the belly, twice. He spilled forward over the
counter like a loose jellyfish. He owned the hash joint. Had . . .
until I shot him in the belly. Now he didn't own anything.

I shot the cook when he came out from in back and then I
shot the cashier. It was early and there were just two customers
and they ran out yelling.

When I got back to the Chevy she was all excited with her
eyes kind of marble shiny and she asked, "How much?"

"Nineteen," I said, driving fast. The Chevy stepped out real
good. We cleared town fast.

"I thought you'd get more." Now she kind of looked like a
slapped kid, all pouty.

"Nineteen is swell," I said. And it was. For 1933 it was swell.

A motor cop started following us and I shot him off his cycle. His hat rolled away into the grass and he had his mouth open, flat on his back, with the flies already at him.

It was July, and real hot. Even this early with the sun just up. I knew it would get a lot hotter.

"Where we goin'?" Hazel asked me.

That was her name. Hazel. She was pretty. Young and pretty. About sixteen. I never ask them how old they are, I just go by what appeals to me. But I'm young too so it figures I like them that way.

I felt real good, all kind of tingly inside, like after you drink champagne. I had it once in Kansas City for New Year's and remember the tingles. Shooting people always makes me feel like that.

"Here." I threw her the gun. "Reload it. There's a box of shells behind the seat."

She shrugged and put in fresh bullets. I took it back and put it away in my coat.

"Where we goin'?" she asked me again.

"To the farm," I said. "It's Ma's birthday. But first I got to find her a present."

Hazel made what sounded like a grunt.

"You got problems with us goin' to Ma's?"

"Naw," she said. "Except that I thought we'd keep movin' after what you done back in that café. All the shooting."

"So what?" I kept my eyes on the road. Nothing to see on either side. Flat Kansas country. "So I shot up some mugs. What's it your business?"

"The cops could be waiting for us at your Ma's."

"Yeah, they could," I said, "except they won't be because they don't know who did the shooting and so that's just a lot of crap."

"Suit yourself." She kind of huddled against the seat with

her arms crossed. She had on a tight yellow blouse that made her tits look good and a tight kid's skirt from school. But her hair was a mess.

"You oughta fix your hair," I told her. "Looks like a rat's been at it."

She put a hand up to her hair, running her fingers through. "The wind messes it," she said. "I'll comb it later."

The wind was pretty strong all right. Across the Kansas flat, blowing the wheat all which way.

"How far to your Ma's? I gotta pee."

"So I'll stop and you can go outside."

I braked the Chevy. The highway was two lanes, quiet and open, with stubbled grass on each side. She could pee in the grass.

"Somebody'll see me," she said.

"Naw they won't," I said. "Just go do it."

She opened the door on her side and slipped out, hiking up her skirt. The wind made a whining sound and the sky was blue like Ma's eyes. Real intense blue. No clouds.

But it might rain by late tonight. That's what the radio said. Clouds could come up and it might rain.

I leaned across the seat. "You done yet?"

"Just hold your horses," she said. About a minute or so later she wiggled back in the seat and slammed the car door.

"I feel a lot better," she said.

We drove on till I found a general store. I pulled the Chevy to a stop in the gravel yard in front and went in.

"Help you, son?" asked this tall gink with squinty eyes and thick glasses. He wore green suspenders.

I picked up a shiny metal iron. Heavy. "Ma needs a new one," I said. "You got any ironing boards? Hers is wore out."

"Sure, you bet," said the squinty gink and he hauled out a

long wooden ironing board for me.

"That'll be three fifty."

"Too much," I said and hit him with the iron. He went down bleeding and didn't say anything else.

I wiped off the iron with a new towel from a stack on the counter, took what he had in the cash register, and left with Ma's presents. She'd be real pleased to get them.

"Why'd you hit that guy?" Hazel wanted to know when I got back to the Chevy.

"Cuz I wanted to," I said. "Why don't you shut your yap."

"I didn't mean nothin'." And she looked pouty again.

"Quit askin' me dumb questions," I said, easing out to the highway.

"Sometimes I just wonder about stuff," she said.

"Well, keep your wonderin' to yourself. Just button it."

"You got a headache or something?"

"Naw, I'm feelin' good."

"Well, you're sure cranky. And when you got a headache you get cranky."

"I just don't like dumb questions is all."

We were almost to Ma's place when they came into sight around a long curve. Three cops in two patrol cars.

"Jeez, it's a roadblock," said Hazel. Her eyes were wide. "And they see us."

"So what?" I tromped hard on the gas and the Chevy jumped forward like a dog in the woods. "Not much of a damn roadblock with just three hick cops. I'll run it."

"They'll shoot! They got a rifle."

"Swell. Just duck down and you'll be okay."

I was moving fast when the bullets started. Most of them missed but one chipped the glass in my side vent and cut my cheek. Stung a little. Then I was on them, bang! Right through, and with me firing from the window.

Got one fat cop. Blew him away like a straw man. The other two ducked down inside their car.

The road curved again. Once we were out of their sight I swung off to a narrow dirt road with lots of trees for cover and heard them go by on the main highway, sirens blasting.

"They'll catch us," said Hazel. "You should not of shot that cop."

"They started it," I said. "Shooting at us. Trying to kill us. Hell, it was self-defense."

"Plus the motor cop you popped earlier," said Hazel. "They hate cop killers."

"So what? I hate cops. That makes us even."

Ma's place was good to see again. Just a plain weathered house with a black tar roof stuck in beside some big oaks with plowed ground behind and a rusty Dodge truck in the driveway. Used to be Pa's before the stroke took him. Ma used it to fetch back groceries from town.

She met us on the porch, smiling. "Well, goodness me, it's you, Hal! How are ya, son?"

"I'm swell, Ma," I said. "This here is Hazel. She's with me."

"Why, land sakes but you're a pretty little thing," Ma said, wiping her palms on her checked apron. Then she shook Hazel's hand.

"Thank you kindly, ma'am," said Hazel, looking sheepish. She didn't get told nice things much about her looks.

"Her hair's messed up," I said.

Hazel patted at it. "The wind," she told Ma. "It's blowin' fierce today."

"Sure is," said Ma. "Now you younguns step on inside. I got some coffee and pie in the kitchen."

That sounded swell. I was real hungry and Ma knew how to bake a pie.

"What kind?" I asked her, going inside. The house looked the same. The big picture of Jesus was still over the mantel.

"Blueberry. Your favorite."

I gave her a hug. "Happy birthday, Ma."

"Gracious!" She lit up like a searchlight. "You went and remembered!"

"Sure did." I gave her a smile. "Got some presents for ya out in the Chevy."

"Well, now, ain't that nice." She seemed real pleased. "Ain't that just the nicest thing!"

We ate Ma's blueberry pie and drank the coffee, and I asked for a second slice. It was like always. Tasted great. And filled me up good. Hazel liked it too.

I got out the iron and the ironing board and brought them inside to Ma. She about had a fit she was so glad to get the stuff. Gave me another hug.

"Ya know," Ma said to Hazel, "Hal here usta be a plain mischief to me. Cuttin' up all the time and gettin' into trouble." She shook her head. "But he always had the looks. Took after his Pa."

She had the family scrapbook spread out on her lap and was showing Hazel some photos of me as a kid. I grabbed it away from her.

"Can it, Ma. Hazel don't wanna see all this crap." I shrugged. "So I was a lousy kid. All kids are lousy, and that's why I'll never have any."

Hazel started to protest about the scrapbook but I shot her a look and she kept shut.

"Look, Ma, we gotta push on," I said.

She seemed kind of pained. "Why the rush? Thought you kids could stay the night."

"Naw, we gotta push on," I said. "Want to make Railston before the weather goes bad. Radio said a storm is due."

"Hotels at Railston cost ya a bundle," Ma said. "You could stay here, go on to town come morning."

I shook my head and nudged Hazel through the pitted screen door ahead of me. "Sorry, but I gotta see a fella in Railston real early tomorrow. Big shot from K.C."

It was a lie, but it got us out with no more argument.

Ma walked us to the Chevy. "You drive careful now, Hal."

"Always, Ma," I said, giving her a final hug. Hazel gave her one too.

"Take care," Ma said, waving at us as we rolled out of the driveway.

We hit Railston by 2 p.m. The Farmers' Bank on the main street was still open.

"I'm gonna take it," I said. "You wait in the car. Keep the motor running. I'll be back in a jiffy."

"This is nuts with all the local law after us," Hazel complained. "It's like we're Bonnie and Clyde."

"Just shut up and keep the motor goin' that's all."

I went inside, walked up to the lady cashier and shot her in the head. Some people screamed and I told them to shut up. It was a hick bank with no guard. I got ninety-two dollars and ten cents. Hotcha! Almost a hundred smacks!

Outside I piled into the Chevy and took off fast. People were yelling behind us.

"You shot somebody else, didn't you?" asked Hazel. "I heard it."

"What I do is none of your goddamn business. If you don't like what I do then you can haul your butt outa this car."

We'd already cleared town and I braked hard, pulled over to the side of the highway and kicked open the passenger door.

"Go on . . . get outa here!"

"Then I will," she said, her face all tight and red. "I surely will."

When she was clear I reached across and yanked the door closed, hit the gas, and took off again.

I saw her in the rear-view mirror, standing there by the side of the road with her yellow blouse hanging out and her hair all messed.

She was nothing. There were plenty of others just like her in Topeka. I wouldn't have any trouble finding another one just as pretty.

I'd have to switch cars in Topeka. Cinch.

Everything was swell. I felt the tingles inside, like bubbles.

It was a good day.

*This story, selected for **The Best of Cemetery Dance**, was inspired by a late-life reading of **Crime and Punishment**, combined with the city-wide proliferation of sad-faced street corner characters bearing "work for food" signs.*

I asked myself: what if I picked up one of these grimy people and took him home? Out of such questions, stories arise, as did "Fyodor's Law."

You'll wince at least once in reading this story. Well, if you don't, I'll be disappointed.

That's my job here: to make you wince.

Fyodor's Law

They were at nearly every street corner in Greater Los Angeles, standing or sitting cross-legged in their ragged, dirt stiffened clothing, their faces stubble-bearded, eyes slack and defeated, clutching crude, hand-lettered cardboard signs:

HOMELESS!

HUNGRY!

WILL WORK FOR FOOD

PLEASE HELP???

GOD BLESS YOU!!!

Today he would help one of them as he had helped many others. He took no credit for this; it was simply his way, his personal contribution. He felt a real sense of pity for them. Society's outcasts. The dispossessed. The lost ones.

Dostoyevsky's children.

The one he selected was standing on the south corner at Topanga Canyon and Ventura, in front of a hardware store. He was very tall, well over six feet, and of indeterminate age.

Under his ragged hat and twist of beard he could be thirty, or forty, or even fifty. They *all* had old faces; they'd lived too long on the dark side, seen too much, experienced too many horrors. The pain of existence etched their skin.

He pulled the long blue Cadillac to a whispered stop at the curb and ran down the passenger window, beckoning to the tall man. "Over here," he called, waving. The sun flashed rainbow colors from the diamond ring on his left hand.

The ragged figure approached the car.

"Get in . . . I have work for you." The driver's name was Conover—James Edward Stanton Conover—and he lived alone in a hillside home on the other side of the Santa Monica Mountains in Bel Air. He was wealthy by inheritance, had no need for work, and although he considered himself a professional artist, had never attempted to sell any of his creations. Every other year he traded in his Cadillac for the latest model. He always drove Cadillacs; his family had never driven anything else. His great-grandfather, in fact, had owned the first Cadillac in Los Angeles.

"You gonna help me, huh, mister?" The bearded man was leaning down to peer inside the car at James Conover.

"Right, I'll help you." Conover opened the passenger door. "Please, get in. We'll drive to my place. I have some work for you."

"I can fix anything," declared the tall man, tossing his hat and grimed knapsack into the seat behind him. "Do your plumbing. Repair your roof. Tile your patio. Weed your garden. Paint or plaster. You name her, mister, and I can do her."

Conover smiled at the man as he put the blue Cadillac into drive, rejoining the eastbound traffic stream along Ventura Boulevard. "You're a regular Jack of all trades," he said.

"*That's* my name," said the ragged man. "Jack. Jack Wilbur."

"How did you acquire all these remarkable skills, Mr. Wilbur?"

"From my Pap," replied Jack Wilbur. "We come here from Tennessee, me an' my Pap, after Ma took sick an' died. My brother an' little sis, they stayed on in Willicut, but we come out here to the Coast, the two of us." He stared at Conover. "Ever hear of Willicut?"

"Can't say that I have."

"It's fifty miles north of Chattanooga. Little bitty runt of a town, but full of good folks. My brother, he owns a feed store back in Willicut. That's how come he stayed there."

"Where's your father now?"

"Pap's in jail," said Jack Wilbur. "He done a violent act, an' they arrested him."

"What kind of violent act?"

"Well, ole Pap, he drinks some. We was in this pool hall in North Hollywood, an' Pap was takin' on whiskey. He gets mean when he drinks, an' pretty soon he's into a bustup with a trucker over one of the pool hall ladies. Killed him, Pap did. Just smashed his head right in."

"And you witnessed this?"

"Sure as hell did. But I couldn't stop what Pap done. All happened too fast. One minute the pair of 'em are yellin' over this blondie, an' the next ole Pap is layin' this pool stick alongside the fella's head. Split it open like you do a canta-loupe. It was a sight, I'll tellya. Blondie was screamin' like she was havin' a fit an' the police come an' hauled Pap off and now he's in jail."

"How did you end up on the street? It would seem that a man with your variegated skills could support himself."

"Well, I sure tried. But unless you work for some company it's tough findin' jobs that pay much. Since I lack me any kinda formal schoolin', no company will take me on. Believe me, mister, I'm no bum by nature. No siree, not Jack Wilbur. Back in Willicut I worked regular from when I was just a nipper, an' I had respect. Nobody called Jack Wilbur a bum in Willicut."

"After your father's incarceration, why didn't you return home—to be with your brother and sister?"

"Naw!" The bearded man shook his head. "I can't go back now. For one thing, I gotta earn enough money to show all them locals I amounted to somethin' worthwhile out here in California. Our family's always had a lotta pride, an' I can't go low-tailin' home like some kinda whipped hound. It's bad enough, what happened to Pap."

"I understand," nodded Conover. "I really do."

They were on the freeway, taking the connector to the southbound 405, headed for Bel Air. The sleek blue car purred along at sixty, smooth and steady.

"Real nice machine you got here," said Jack Wilbur. "I plan to buy me one a'these soon as I get back on my feet so to speak."

"You seem confident that it will happen."

"Betcha. Man like me, with all my talents, I'm fair bound to come out a winner. Just a matter of time. An' I'm only thirty, so I *got* me some time."

"I take it you've never been married."

"Nope—but I come real close once. There was this sweet little thing over to Haines—that's near Willicut—an' she just about roped me for sure, but I slipped away clean. Lucky I got shut of her when I did. Hell's bells, marriage should be for when you're ready to settle down and raise a flock a'kids." He chuckled. "Me, I'm a natural born ramblin' man. Been through sixteen states. That's another reason I don't want to go back to Willicut. It's what's on the other side of the hill that always takes my fancy."

"I admire your spirit," said Conover.

"What kinda work you got for me?"

"I live on a steep hillside," said Conover. "Lots of thick, fast-growing brush and trees up there. Dangerous in the fire season. I need this brush cut back from the house."

"I can do that easy," said the bearded man. He hesitated. "But I got no cuttin' tools. You got those?"

Conover nodded. "Everything you'll need is in the garage. Don't worry."

Jack Wilbur grinned. "Hell's bells, mister, that's one thing I *never* do—is worry. With me, things always have a way of workin' out fine."

And Conover repeated: "I admire your spirit."

James Conover's angular, flat-roofed, two-story house, at the top of Bel Air road, hovered at the edge of a heavily brushed canyon like some huge stone-and-glass animal. Below the overhanging cast-steel deck the ground fell away in a steep drop that made Jack Wilbur dizzy.

"Geez!" he muttered, peering down. "Aren't you scared?"

"Of what?" asked Conover, standing beside him on the deck.

"Of this whole shebang ending up at the bottom of the canyon! I mean, a big quake could be murder."

"This structure is supported by steel construction beams sunk deep into granite, considerably below the surface soil. There's no need to fear earthquakes, let me assure you."

"Well, I'd say you got some guts, livin' in a place like this. Fine for an eagle maybe, or a buzzard."

Conover smiled thinly. "I happen to appreciate the view. On a clear day you can see forever."

Wilbur shrugged; it was apparent he didn't recognize the reference. " 'Bout time for me to get crackin' on that job you mentioned."

"No rush," said Conover. "I spend a lot of hours alone up here and I could use some company. How about a drink before beginning your labors?"

Wilbur looked uncertain. "Pretty early in the day for booze," said the tall man. "I usually don't start till the sun's down."

"Then make an exception," urged Conover. "I have some excellent imported brandy. Aged to perfection." He saw Jack frown. "You *do* drink brandy?"

Again, Wilbur shrugged, uncertain. "Hard whiskey's more my style."

"All right, then, I have some Black Irish that should be suitable." He moved to the tinted glass door leading into the den and slid it back. "Please . . ." He waved Wilbur inside.

The den was richly paneled in carved oak with a fully stocked bar at the far end. Conover nodded toward a leather-topped stool as he moved behind the bar to fix their drinks.

Jack Wilbur scowled at his image in the bar mirror, rubbing a slow hand along his bearded chin. "Boy, I look kinda ragged. Need me a trim."

"Here you go, Jack," said Conover, placing a glass of Black Irish whiskey in front of Wilbur. He walked around the bar with his own drink, moving to a deep red-leather couch. "Let's make ourselves comfortable."

They settled into the couch and Conover, after a sip of whiskey, asked Wilbur if he had ever met any professional artists.

"You mean guys that do pictures?"

"In general, yes."

"Well, I never met none personal. Artists don't show up much in Willicut, I guess. Pap told me once that when he was in Chicago, he shook hands with the comics guy who did *Dick Tracy*."

Conover smiled. "If you'll wait here," he said, "I have something to show you."

He walked out of the den and returned with a thick scrapbook handsomely bound in levant morocco. He placed the book, unopened, on the coffee table in front of Jack Wilbur. Then he resumed his seat on the couch, taking another sip of Black Irish.

"What's in there?" asked Wilbur. "Pictures of your family?"

"Not exactly," Conover replied. "But they are photos. Of my art."

"So *you're* an artist, huh?"

"Correct." Conover smiled. "But not in any conventional sense of the term."

"What does that mean?"

"It means I'm not a painter or a sketch artist. I do montages."

Wilbur looked confused. "Mon what? I never heard of 'em."

"A montage is made up of various separate components. The artist uses these components to achieve a particular design. Actual three-dimensional objects are often utilized in the overall work."

"You're way over my head," said Jack Wilbur.

"You'll understand exactly what I'm referring to when I show you the photos."

"Well, I'm not much for art an' that's a fact. Never been in no museum." He hesitated. "Do these . . . mantoges of yours . . . do they hang in museums?"

"No, I destroy the originals after I photograph them," said Conover. "They exist only in this book."

"Well, I admit you got me curious. Let's have a look at 'em."

"In due course," Conover told him. "First, I must explain certain things."

"What things?" asked Jack Wilbur, taking a solid belt of whiskey.

"Let me begin by outlining a unique personal philosophy." He leaned forward, eyes bright, excited. "Have you ever heard of Dostoyevsky?"

"Nope. He an artist, too?"

"Indeed, yes—and a very great one—but his art was that of the printed word. Fyodor Mikhailovich Dostoyevsky. Eighteen twenty one to eighteen eighty-one. Critics have called him Russia's greatest novelist."

"Russian, huh?" Wilbur shook his head. "No wonder I never heard of the guy. Hell, the only book writer I know about is Ernie Hemingway an' I never actual read anything of his—but how I know about him is because of his boozing. He sure loved to get smashed, Ole Ernie did."

"True enough. Many great writers have fallen prey to the evils of alcohol."

Jack held up his whiskey glass, now three-quarters empty. "If this stuff is evil, then I guess I'm one bad dude." Grinning, he took another swallow.

"Of course, a multitude of critics have attempted to define the essence of Dostoyevsky's work, but the most perceptive analysis comes from a gentleman whose name I fail to recall at the moment. His words, however, are very clear in my memory: 'The extremes of man's nature, his spiritual duality, the conflict between conventional morals and the overwhelming urge to move beyond such constrictions, forms the core of all of Dostoyevsky's major novels.' Beautifully put, I'd say."

"This kinda talk is givin' me a headache," declared Jack Wilbur.

Conover smiled. "Bear with me, Jack. There's a point here that applies directly to both of us—but I have to reach it in my own way. Will you indulge me?"

"Go ahead," said Wilbur.

"Dostoyevsky's greatest work, in my opinion, is the novel he published in eighteen sixty-six, *Crime and Punishment.*"

"The title sounds okay," admitted Wilbur. "You do a crime, you get punished for it—like my Pap."

"The novel's lead character," continued Conover, "is an embittered scholar named Raskolnikov. He murders two women, one of them for money. At least that's what he thinks is his motive: However, money is not Raskolnikov's true reason for the crime. In fact, he hides the stolen loot and never profits from it."

"That's crazy," declared Jack Wilbur. "If he went to all the trouble of knockin' off some dame for her dough, then why didn't he spend it? Sounds like the guy was a real dummy."

"On the contrary, he was a brilliant man," said Conover. "His violent action perfectly reflected the author's personal philosophy. It was through Raskolnikov that Dostoyevsky developed what I choose to call 'Fyodor's Law.' You know, when the novel appeared, it was considered quite controversial. It shocked many people."

"How come?"

"Dostoyevsky boldly declared that truly extraordinary people are not bound by conventional moral standards. He wrote of a higher 'law of nature' unknown to the untutored mass of humanity. This law permits the extraordinary individual to commit violent acts, including murder, in order to advance beyond, to transcend ordinary boundaries."

"That's a hell of a thing to put in people's heads."

"Allow me to quote directly from memory," Conover continued, ignoring Wilbur's negative comment. "Raskolnikov speaks of a 'right to crime,' and adds: 'If such a one is forced, for the sake of his idea, to wade through blood, he can find within his conscience, a *sanction* for wading through blood.' The author, of course, was not advocating such extreme behavior for everyone—only for the truly extraordinary individual."

"Horseshit," muttered Jack Wilbur.

Undeterred, Conover went on: "If the individual is clever enough, his actions will never be discovered by the law. For one thing, a dead body is the primary proof of murder. But what if the body simply vanishes?" He spread his hands. "No corpse, no provable crime."

"Bodies don't vanish."

"Ah, but they *can,*" argued Conover. "All one need do is saw the corpse into small parts and then burn each part to a fine grey ash. Quite simple, actually."

Jack Wilbur stared intently at him. "This is pretty heavy stuff," he said slowly.

"It's time to open my scrapbook," said Conover. He flipped back the heavy cover to reveal, within the book's pages, a variety of color photos—of human body parts arranged on brightly painted boards in bizarre designs.

"My art," Conover declared proudly. "Unfortunately, for obvious reasons, I am unable to preserve the originals. Sadly, I am forced to burn each montage after I have completed it. But at least I have this book of photographs. Arms, legs, hands, ears, noses . . . they all comprise my basic artistic materials."

"Christ!" breathed Jack Wilbur, staring at one of the photos. "That's a guy's dick!"

"Yes," nodded Conover. "I am sometimes able to utilize genitalia to splendid effect. But *every* body part is potentially usable." He pointed to another photo. "Here we have a loop of bowel tract, actually part of the small intestine, surrounding a freshly-severed heart. Quite original, don't you think?"

Jack Wilbur stood up, backing away from his host. "What I think, mister, is that you're one sick son of a bitch!"

"Sit down, Jack," said Conover sharply. "I laced that drink of yours with a potent pharmaceutical drug that will render you totally helpless within a very short period."

"I don't believe it," said Wilbur.

"Trust me. I'm quite adept at this by now. Very soon your lungs will begin to tighten. With every breath they will expand less, restricting the oxygen available to you. Then black spots will appear before your eyes as you gasp for air. You'll fall to the floor and lie there for a minute or two, conscious but unable to move. And then your heart will stop and it will all be over."

"You plan to cut me up in pieces an' use me for one of your damn pictures?"

"Precisely," nodded Conover. "I'm actually doing you a service—helping you to make something special out of your otherwise miserable life. You shall serve the cause of true artistic expression. A noble end to your mundane existence."

"How can you just go around killing people?" gasped Jack Wilbur. His skin was red and flushed with heat.

"After the first time it becomes quite easy. One's first murder is always somewhat disturbing. Now all I feel is a sense of exhilaration." He checked his wristwatch. "Time's up, Jack. The poison kicks in very suddenly. No use your attempting to fight it. Just let . . ." He stood up eyes wide. "Just . . . let it . . ."

James Conover staggered, clutching at his throat. He choked, gasping for breath. Then he fell to his knees, toppling sideways to the polished peg floor of the den. Lying on his back, he stared sightlessly at the ceiling, conscious but totally paralyzed.

"Well, Mr. Conover," said Jack Wilbur as he removed the fallen man's wallet and slipped the diamond ring from the middle finger of his left hand, "your back was to me when you put that stuff in my glass, but I could see what you was doing in the mirror. When you went to fetch your book of sicko pictures I switched glasses. Guess the joke's on you, huh?"

There was no physical response from Conover, but Jack caught a faint flicker of shocked understanding in the dying man's eyes. Then they began glazing over. Conover had, at best, another few seconds of life.

Jack Wilbur bent over him, leaning close, smiling. "Fuck you, Mr. Conover," he said softly.

He removed the man's car keys and gold wristwatch, walked out to the shiny blue Cadillac, and motored away down the hill, whistling.

The sun was very bright and the Los Angeles air was smogless and sweet.

Jack Wilbur felt "truly extraordinary."

Originally, this story was aimed for a Batman anthology, but there were restrictions on the plot line so I felt that the story would be better served as an original.

It deals with the question: how does an ordinary man end up as a masked crime fighter? What as a Batman story might have been nothing more than another fast-action adventure ends up as a character study.

I've always been fascinated with super-heroes. As a boy, growing up in Kansas City, I created my own line of masked crime fighters, setting them up on my desk as paper cutouts, and drawing their adventures in crude comic-book format.

"Die, Clown, Die!" reflects that early passion of mine.

Die, Clown, Die!

I've never been much for holidays. Mostly, they just depress me. Christmas hasn't been any good since I was a kid. And even then it wasn't so great. Now it's just a day to get through. Easter was always a drag. Who the hell cared about looking for colored eggs? My parents used to get very drunk— and very loud—on New Year's Eve, so I've got some bad memories there. Fourth of July is okay. I've always liked fireworks. But the one holiday I really *hate* is St. Valentine's Day. And I have a damn good reason.

My brother was murdered on St. Valentine's Day.

I've never been married, so I've got no kids of my own. And no other brothers or sisters. Maybe my parents loved me, but they never took the trouble to show it. I never cared much for either of them. My fault maybe, the fact that we just didn't communicate. Danny was the only person I ever really loved. My "big brother," Danny Gregson. He was only two years older, but he was a kind of god to me—a brother to idolize. Never had any school friends.

It was just the two of us, in Oakland, California, growing up together in the 1930s—him born in '26 and me in '28. Mom told us she and Pop couldn't afford any more kids. "You take care of Bobby," Mom would say to my brother. "He's small. He gets picked on."

And I was—and did. I was a pimply runt of a boy, short for my age, while Danny was strong and tall and good-looking from the start. He could do everything I couldn't: climb the highest trees, leap across roofs, outrun any kid in the neighborhood, do cartwheels, box and arm-wrestle. And he was great at school sports. You name it, he was great at it. Not me, though. I wore glasses and always had a cold and was plain lousy at all sports. It was a world I didn't fit into. I couldn't hit a baseball or sink a basket and I was way too small for football. (Naturally, Danny was team captain.)

The bigger kids were all afraid of him. They'd be ragging me, making fun of my jug ears or my big feet and Danny would come along and light into them like a whirlwind. Got so they left me alone because if they didn't, they ended up with a black eye and some loose teeth. Courtesy of Danny Gregson.

It's like I've said, he was a god to me, the only god I ever knew personally. That's why his death hit me so hard. Almost half a century ago and sometimes I still wake up at night crying out his name. We'd still be close as ever if he'd lived. I know it. And things would have been different. My whole existence would have been different if Danny had lived. I wouldn't be alone now with nothing but books for company and I would never have become a writer, that's for damn sure. Writers are offbeat, isolated people. You turn *inside* yourself when you write. You don't live in the real world, only the world inside your head. It's kind of spooky, being a writer.

Danny would have done great things as a man, and he would have taken me right along with him. I'd be rich by now. Own a big white two-story house on Nob Hill instead of a dark, sleazy apartment here in Hollywood. Christ! Hollywood's become Freak City—and I guess I'm one of the freaks.

So I write. Mostly I do magazine work on assignment. I come up with an idea for a special feature piece, get an okay on my idea from an editor, then go out and write it.

That's how I set up the interview with old man Wainwright. I told T. J. Shaw, the author of *Legends*, that I wanted to do a feature profile on Wainwright. Shaw was skeptical; he was convinced that it was impossible to reach the old man. I told him not to worry, that I had a way.

No doubt about it, the old boy *was* a legendary character. Back in the 1930s he'd been the real-life model for Nightman, the world-famous comic-book hero. The Crime Crusher. But Wainwright's full story had never been told. Patchwork pieces had been written on him, but no one had ever been able to reach him for an interview. Not for decades, that is. He was a rich recluse, sealed off from the world behind the walls of his big estate up-coast near San Francisco. He'd been there all those years, and no one had ever seen him leave the place—not once since 1943. (That was a very fateful year in my life. Danny had been murdered on St. Valentine's Day, 1943.)

So how did *I* get to the old man? Why did the legendary Benjamin Clarke Wainwright agree to grant me a personal interview? It was the letter I wrote to him (he didn't have a phone, had never allowed one to be installed in his mansion). I wrote something in the letter that made him want to see me. I was about to reach him when no one else could. For the first exclusive interview in forty-five years.

It was going to be memorable.

The handwritten letter I got from him—the one I showed T. J. Shaw to notch the assignment—told me exactly how to reach his place (over a private road), how many times to honk my horn at the gate, and how many times to blink my lights. I was instructed to arrive there at midnight sharp, and he told me precisely where to find a hidden key to the mansion's front door. I was to let myself in, verbally identify myself, and then wait for him to appear. And, of course, I was to come alone. No other writers. No photographers. Just me. Alone. At midnight.

"Sounds like a visit to Dracula's castle," Shaw had declared after reading the letter. "Maybe you should take along some garlic." He chuckled. "And a sharp wooden stake!"

"So he's eccentric. All I care about is the fact that he's agreed to see me."

Shaw grunted. "Whatever you told him, it sure did the trick. This ought to make one hell of a story. Come back here with an in-depth interview and I'll tack a bonus onto your check."

Shaw didn't know what I'd put in my letter to the old man, and I'd refused to tell him. It was strictly my business. The words I'd written had earned me a ticket inside Benjamin C. Wainwright's private world.

The drive up-coast from Los Angeles took me almost eight hours. I didn't hurry because I had a lot to think about.

By the time I'd located Wainwright's private road two

miles inland from the ocean town of Bodega Bay it was already close to midnight. A swirling fog reduced vision, and the road was giving me a bumpy ride. Its packed-gravel surface hadn't been maintained and my little Toyota jolted through deep potholes and bounced over rock-strewn sections, ridged by wild tree roots. Obviously the old boy didn't care about the condition of the road because *he* never used it. But at least I was making progress, slow but sure.

The fog's damp chill was beginning to penetrate the car's interior. It smelled of brine from the sea—a sharp, rusty odor. I switched on the dash heater, which helped.

The road seemed endless and I began to worry about being late. The old man's letter had specified that I reach the gate at "exactly twelve."

Maybe the damn gate wouldn't open after midnight. When you're dealing with a bizarre eccentric like Wainwright, you can't count on anything. So, despite the lousy road conditions and the lack of visibility, I speeded up. It was a risk I had to take.

Five minutes later the rising shape of a tall iron gate loomed in the path of my probing headlights. I stopped, sounded my horn three times, then blinked the lights twice.

Slowly, with a shriek of tortured metal, the gate swung open.

I drove inside, along a shorter (and smoother) access road, until I was able to make out the high Gothic towers of Wainwright House through a swirling gap in the fog.

I braked to a stop in front of the entrance, cut my engine and lights, and sat there thinking that Shaw had been right; this was a hell of a lot like visiting Castle Dracula.

I got out of the Toyota; the slammed door rang like a pistol shot in the fog-thick stillness. I looked up at the towering bulk of wood and stone. Darkness shrouded the sprawling Gothicspired mansion. The windows were lightless. I could see no evidence of interior life.

The door key (heavy black metal, rust-pebbled) was just where Wainwright's letter said it would be—under a loose board at the edge of the wide stone entrance steps. The key was cold against the palm of my hand. I mounted the steps to the door, fitted the key into a blackened slot, twisted, and the carved wooden door swung inward with a sound like cats screaming.

I stepped into a vast, marble-floored entry hall, faintly illumined by four sputtering, white-wax candles, set in high wall brackets. Not having a phone in the place was crazy enough—but *candles!*

Directly ahead of me a wide stairway curved upward into second-story blackness. I remembered my instructions: I was to identify myself, "in a clear voice."

I felt like a stage actor facing an empty theater. "I'm Bob Gregson," I called out. My words kicked echoes back from the somber walls.

I waited. Nothing. No sound or movement. Where was the old man? Maybe dead of a heart attack from the shock of my letter.

Then I looked upward. A light was descending the stairs, flickering against faded gold wall tapestries and gilt-framed oil paintings (of Wainwright's ancestors?).

I was about to meet a legend.

A gaunt figure slowly materialized on the stairway. He reached the last stair, moved slowly toward me across the marble floor. Limping. A thick black cane in one hand, a candle in the other. The wavering light from the candle flame threw the old man's face into sharp relief, accenting the hollows of his skull; deep wrinkles cut into his skin like wounds. He looked far older than his seventy-five years—a time-ravaged crone of a man.

"Benjamin Wainwright?" I asked.

"Who the hell *else* would live in a tomb like this?" He nodded toward a side hall. "There's brandy in the library. We can talk there."

I followed as his tapping cane reverberated along the dim hallway. Our passage was a long one, with the hall stretching forward into the depths of the house. Wainwright suddenly swayed, stumbling against me, clutching at my shoulder for support.

"Are you all right?"

"Yes, yes . . . It's just that I . . . I'm not used to walking much anymore. I must apologize for my awkwardness."

"Forget it," I said.

We moved on down the hall.

In Wainwright's cavernous library, the snapping flames from a deep stone fireplace helped warm me up a little—and a snifter of good Napoleon brandy finished the job.

I was beginning to feel human again. The oppressive dreamlike atmosphere of Wainwright House was quickly achieving a livable reality.

We were seated in two large red velour chairs, close to the fire. The old man looked up from lowered brows, fixing me with an eagle's glare. "Do you know why I have allowed you to enter my house?"

"I know."

He continued to glare at me, white hair forming a thin halo over his lowered head.

"I don't give interviews," he said. "Don't allow people to come here. You're the first outsider I've seen in more than forty years."

"How do you get food?"

"It's brought in. A servant delivers it. Then he leaves. I don't let anyone stay here at night."

"Hell of a life," I said.

His glare intensified. "It's *my* life, and you'd be no part of it except for—" He hesitated. "Except for that last sentence in your letter."

He held up the letter I'd sent, punching a withered finger at the words, repeating them aloud: " 'I'm Danny's brother.' " He tossed the letter aside. "Is it true?"

"Yes," I said. "It's true."

"Show me proof," he rasped. "I must be absolutely certain of your identity before we talk."

I reached into an inner pocket of my London Fog topcoat and took out an 8-by-10 manila envelope. I gave it to him. "Here's your proof."

He opened the envelope with shaking fingers, drawing out the contents. Documents and photos. Leaning closer to the fire, he carefully examined each item. Sherlock Holmes couldn't have done a better job. Then he returned everything to the envelope and handed it to me.

"Well," I said, "do you believe me now?"

The old man scrubbed at his eyes; tears glittered against his cheeks. His voice was a strained whisper: "You're Danny's brother." He raised his veined hands in a helpless gesture. "God, how I loved him!"

"We both did," I said. "Danny was the most important person in my life."

Wainwright paced in front of the stone fireplace. He sighed, a racking sound of anguish. "I haven't spoken his name in all these years. To anyone." Another sigh. "But to-night . . . I *want* to talk about him . . . and about the inhuman devil who killed him."

"That's good," I said, "because I have a lot of questions to

112

ask. No one else can give me the answers I need. Okay?"

Wainwright nodded. "I'll answer anything about Danny."

He poured more brandy into my glass. I didn't mind. Nothing better than brandy on a cold, wet night. Then he sat down next to me again, staring into the fire.

"Let's start with how you became a role model for Nightman," I said quietly. "Before you met my brother."

"You know the story, I'm sure. It was in all the papers back in '43, at the time Danny was—"

"I want to hear it from you, *your* version of what happened. Newspapers get things wrong."

I eased back in the chair with my drink, watching his eyes as he talked.

He had a lot to say.

"It began early in 1938. I'd just turned twenty-five and I was bored with life. This was in New York, and there was a lot of crime in town. All the big cities were seedbeds for crime, just as they are today. You didn't have to look to find it."

He hesitated, gathering his thoughts. I kept watching him, saying nothing. This was what I had come for.

"I was an avid reader of pulp magazines back then," the old man declared. "Four years earlier, in 1934, I'd grown fond of a character called the Black Bat—a crime-fighting hero featured in *Black Bat Detective Magazine*. I don't remember who the author was."

"Murray Leinster," I said. "His real name was Will Jenkins."

Wainwright canted his head and a faint smile twisted his lips. "You *do* know the story, don't you?"

"Go ahead."

"So . . . in '38, bored out of my mind, I got this wild idea. Why not rig myself up in a costume and become a genuine crime fighter? With a mask, so nobody would know my real identity. More I thought about the idea, the more excited I got." The old man's eyes shone in the firelight. "Life suddenly took on purpose and meaning. I bought a black Halloween outfit from a costume shop in lower Manhattan, then made myself a cape out of a black silk bed sheet. Then I made a hood, with eyeholes cut into it, to fit over my head. By the time I'd added boots and black gloves and strapped a holstered .45 around my waist, I was something to see. I thought I'd laugh at myself in the mirror, wearing this kind of getup, but I looked menacing. And the gun was loaded—although I didn't plan on shooting anybody."

"And you went crook hunting in that black outfit." It was a statement, not a question.

"Sure did. The first night out I caught two punks robbing a grocery in Queens. When they left that store with the cash, I leaped from the shadows and scared the shit out of them!" A dry chuckle. "Knocked their heads together, tied them up with a length of clothesline and phoned the police. When they got there they found my note pinned to one of the punks."

"Saying what?"

"Note said, 'Courtesy of Nightman!' " Again the chuckle. "It made all the papers the next morning."

"So that started your career as a crime fighter?"

"Sure did. For about three months that year I played this role. Caught me maybe a dozen crooks. That's when the *New York Times* did their editorial on me."

"I remember seeing it," I said. "They condemned you as a vigilante, but applauded the results you were getting."

"That's when Ray Ruric got into it," Wainwright declared. "He'd seen the editorial. Ray was a young artist working in New York, drawing for *Hero Comics* . . . *Carnival Comics* . . . magazines like that. Superman had appeared in *Action Comics* in June of that year and comic-book editors were looking for more superheroes. The field was wide open for new characters. And that's when Ruric got the idea of contacting me."

"But how did he reach you? Your identity wasn't known."

"He did the only thing he *could* do—put an ad in the Personals column of every paper in New York, asking Nightman to contact him. His ad said, 'Confidential. No police.' Gave a phone number—and I answered."

"But why? You were risking arrest."

"I was curious. I wanted to find out who wanted to see me and what was behind it." The old man smiled thinly. "Hell, I was full of ginger in those days. Wasn't afraid of anything or anybody."

"So you and Ruric got together?"

"Right. He came to see me with a writer friend of his, Will Martin. Told me they wanted to use me as the model for a new comic-book character they planned to call Nightman. They wanted details on how I did what I did. Said they'd cut me in on the profits."

"And what did you say?"

"I told them to keep their money. My daddy was rich and he'd left plenty to me. I didn't want cash, I just wanted the kick of seeing a version of myself in the comic books. I said I'd cooperate all the way."

"And you did."

"Right. Showed them how I'd rigged the engine of my car, souped it up for better performance. You need a fast car when you're hunting criminals."

"The Rocket. Did you call it that?"

"No, no . . . that was Ruric's name for the car. With a spaceship on the hood or some other nonsense. I just had a Cadillac, a real fast Cadillac sedan. But it was black. Not as easy to spot a black car at night."

"What was next?"

"In the mail I got this copy of the June 1939 issue of *Carnival Comics*, and there he was—'Nightman by Ray Ruric'! Cape, black hood, and all. Ruric had even used a variant of my name."

"Benjamin Wainwright became Wain Bentley."

"Right. I got a big kick out of the whole thing."

"You left New York that summer, didn't you?"

He nodded. "Moved to California, here to this house. My father willed it to me when he died."

"And where, exactly, did you meet Danny?"

"I used to go to a gym twice a week in downtown San Francisco. On Market Street. To keep myself in real good shape. I'd box and swim and jump rope, do some weights—that sort of thing. Turns out Danny was there, at this same gym. Working out. He was just a kid then."

"He was thirteen," I said tightly.

"Right. Thirteen. But with a good, firm, muscled body for a kid. He had a copy of *Carnival Comics*, with Nightman in it, and we got to talking. I told him it was based on me, that I was a real-life crime fighter."

"Did he believe you?"

"Not at first. Not till I showed him some clippings from New York. Kept them in my wallet. That got him real excited and he asked me if I needed any help. Could he join me in fighting criminals? Now, since I'd moved to California, I hadn't done any night fighting, but I'd seen plenty of crime flourishing, especially around the city's Barbary Coast area. So I thought, Sure, I could use some help. Two are more effective than one."

"The deadly duo."

He chuckled again. "Right. Well, Danny needed a costume—so we got one together, with a cape and a little domino mask and black tights and a yellow tunic. Had an M sewn onto it."

"For Moonboy," I supplied.

"Exactly. That's the name Danny selected for his mystery identity. I made him swear to keep the whole thing a secret. I remember him asking, 'Can't I even tell Bobby?' And I said that he must tell *no* one. Not if he was serious about wanting to help me fight crime. He gave me his word."

"And he *kept* it," I said. "I never knew about it. Not until—his death."

"More brandy?" asked Wainwright.

"No, I've had enough."

"Then I hope you won't mind . . ." And he poured another for himself, holding the glass up to allow firelight to play through the brandy's amber depths.

"What happened then . . . after Danny had his costume?"

"We formed a special game plan. Decided to go out only on holiday nights: New Year's Eve, Fourth of July, Halloween, Christmas Eve . . . that sort of thing."

"Why just holidays?"

"There's much more crime on a holiday. People get careless. Drink too much. That's when they're ripe for criminals. Besides, in San Francisco I wanted to limit my activities somewhat. It isn't as large as New York and I had to maintain a lower profile to keep from being arrested. Our 'Holiday Plan' was the answer."

"Was Danny good—on the street with you?"

"Absolutely. He was lithe and quick, and used a slingshot to marvelous effect. Knocked down one gunman from twenty yards away, in almost total darkness. And he could fight like a wildcat."

"When did Ray Ruric find out about Danny?"

"We kept in touch by phone. I was giving him tips on the Nightman character. When I told him I had a young associate, he got all excited again—and suddenly Moonboy evolved as a companion for Nightman. They changed his name—from Danny Gregson to Greg Dickson—and he made his debut in *Carnival Comics* in 1940."

"And how did Danny feel about it?"

"He was delighted. Said it made him famous in a kind of mysterious way."

Then I reached the heart of our conversation. "I want to know about the Fiend," I said, the words ominous and heavy in the firelit room.

A tense moment of silence from Wainwright. His eyes narrowed; his hands were fisted. "That murderous devil!" he said softly.

"Tell me about him."

"He wasn't real. Not at the start he wasn't," declared Wainwright. "At first he was only a face on a circus poster, a clown's smiling face. But the face was evil, with a twisted smile. Finally I took this poster and sent it to Ray Ruric with a note saying 'If Nightman needs a villain to fight, here he is!' Next thing I knew, the Nightman had an archenemy, a fellow with purple hair and a pointed chin and a satanic smile. And that's how the Fiend was born."

"When did you encounter the real-life character?"

"Not until 1942. On the Fourth of July. Danny was ill and didn't go out on our run that night."

"He had the flu," I said. "Stayed in bed at our place in Oakland. With me taking care of him."

"Well, that was the night I met the Fiend. I was checking a broken window in a large department store in the Marina district when this tall figure lunged at me from the shadows, waving a knife with a really wicked-looking blade. I was astonished to see him because he looked *exactly* like he did in the comic books. Quite fearsome, a horror of a man. I was lucky to escape with my life that night."

"You're telling me that some local crackpot had decided

to imitate the comic-book character?"

"Yes. Obviously."

"Let's get to the night Danny was killed: St. Valentine's Day, 1943. I want to hear it from you . . . about how he died."

Wainwright was in his chair by the fire again; now he leaned forward, toward me, as if reaching out for an emotional contact.

"Danny and I were on a stakeout, watching a fur shop we had reason to believe was going to be hit that night. I heard a noise inside the shop. I left Danny in the car, to keep an eye on the front in case someone came out that way, while I went around back."

"And that's when you encountered the Fiend?"

"Exactly. He had a big automatic and he surprised me as I approached the shop's rear door. He jammed that gun into my stomach—and I looked into his painted face, dead white in the moonlight. His carmined lips were pulled back in that devil's smile of his."

"Why didn't he kill you?"

"Because he wanted me to watch him kill Danny. He knew that would be worse than death for me."

"Tell me exactly what happened from that point forward," I said levelly. "Every detail."

"After I'd been gone for ten minutes, Danny got worried and showed up at the rear of the shop. I tried to warn him, started to shout at him, but the Fiend slammed the barrel of the gun across my throat—and I could hardly breathe. Then he leaped past me and began firing at Danny. Three shots. The last bullet drove straight through Danny's heart."

Silence between us. Just the sound of the flames crackling in the hearth; a log fell in a thumping shower of sparks.

"What happened after that?"

"The Fiend vanished, just melted into the night shadows,

leaving me alone with Danny. I felt for the pulse at his neck. But there was none. He was dead. I was numb, horrified; I didn't want to go on living without Danny. That's how much I loved him. But I wouldn't give the Fiend the satisfaction of my suicide—so I got Danny's body to the car, drove to the nearest police station and carried him inside. Told them the whole story."

"And that's when it all came out in the papers—about you being the model for Nightman . . . and Danny for Moonboy."

"Yes, I told them everything. The game was over. It ended that night—in Danny's blood."

"Why weren't you arrested?"

"I had committed no crimes."

"You acted as a vigilante. That's a crime."

"They had no direct proof of my having broken the law."

"And the cops believed you when you told them about this murderous creep made up to look like the Fiend?"

"As you know, from the news accounts of that night, there were two witnesses to back up my story. An elderly couple who happened to be passing the fur shop when the shooting took place. They saw the Fiend clearly before he fled."

"Joergans was the name," I recalled.

"Yes, that was it. Mr. and Mrs. Arthur Joergans."

"Why didn't they call the police?"

"Oh, they did. But it took them a while to locate a phone booth. By the time a patrol car got there, I'd driven away with Danny's body."

"And that ended things for you?"

"Yes. I became a recluse. Just shut myself away from the world in this house. I've been here ever since. Here with the memory of that awful night alive in my mind. I've relived that shooting a thousand times!"

"And what became of the Fiend?"

"He disappeared. Vanished utterly. I'd give my life to find him." Wainwright's closed fists were white at the knuckles; he stood facing the fire, staring into the flames, breathing heavily.

"I know where he is," I said.

The old man spun toward me. "Where? Tell me *where!*"

"He's here. Hiding in this house."

Wainwright picked up his heavy black cane. He rifled his gaze toward the doorway, brows drawn across the bright fierceness of his eyes. "By God, lead me to him! I'm an old man now, but I can still destroy the creature that murdered Danny!"

"I think we might do a better job with this," I said, removing a .38 from the pocket of my topcoat.

I walked to the far corner of the library, scanned a row of morocco-bound volumes, pulled the last one free of the shelf. As I did, the entire section swung back, to reveal an inner room.

Wainwright looked astonished. "There . . . all this time," he whispered. "And I never knew!"

"We'll need some light," I said.

He took a copper candleholder from the desk, held it high. The flame cast a band of wavering light into the hidden room.

I stepped inside, the gun poised, Wainwright beside me.

"He's not here," the old man said.

"Oh, yes he is." I moved to a dressing table with a wide mirror above it. On the table: a large leather case. I tapped a finger against it.

Wainwright stared at me.

I nodded toward a chair in front of the table. "Now," I said. "Show him to me."

He sighed, placing the candle on the table. Then he put the cane aside and sat down before the dust-clouded mirror.

He opened the leather case, lowered his head, and began a series of quick movements.

When he raised his head again, he wore a garish purple wig and his skin was smeared with clown-white greasepaint, his chin pointed, his nose hooked. Then he smiled: the Fiend's smile. The effect was monstrous.

"How did you know where to find me?" he asked. Even his voice had changed. It was much smoother, deadlier, with a tone of oiled menace behind each word.

I kept the .38 steady in my hand, aimed at his head. "Last month, when I went back to visit the old neighborhood in Oakland, they were tearing up the block, clearing it for a new shopping center. Poking around through the ruins of our house, I found a notebook."

"Ah," said the clown-faced man. "And it belonged to Danny?"

"Yes. It was a kind of diary. In a section near the end of the notebook he wrote of finding a hidden room behind a bookcase in your library. And he wrote about the leather makeup case."

"Then you must understand why he had to die," said the Fiend. "He had discovered *me*. And Wainwright didn't want Danny to know about me. He didn't want anyone to know."

"*You're* Wainwright, damn you!"

"Perhaps," he said softly. "A part of me lives within the old man. But Benjamin Wainwright is a weak, sentimental fool. He still grieves for that worthless boy."

My jaw muscles tightened. "All right, let's play your sick little game. Tell me why Danny continued to come here after discovering the truth about you. Why?"

The reply was tinged with cold contempt. "Because he adored Wainwright, of course. Haven't you figured it out by now . . . about the two of them? They were lovers!"

I was stunned. The words cut at me like jagged stones. It was simply a thing I had never considered—never *allowed* myself to consider.

"You're one sick son of a bitch!" I said.

And I squeezed the trigger of the .38 three times.

It clicked emptily.

The grotesque clown smile stretched wider. "When Wainwright stumbled against you in the hallway, he managed to pluck the gun from your topcoat pocket. When he slipped it back again, it was empty. Sometimes the old fool is helpful after all."

"I came here to kill you," I said softly. "And I will. Even if I have to do it with my bare hands."

And I went for him.

He twisted away from me, snatching at the heavy black cane. A hiss of metal, as he drew a long-bladed sword from the cane's hollow interior. It glittered, sharp and deadly, in the candlelight.

I took a quick step back from him, my eyes on the length of razored steel.

The Fiend's laugh was chilling. "You should read the comics," he declared. "I first used this sword cane against Nightman in 'Die, Clown, Die!' in 1940. I would have killed him with it, too, but that foul boy intervened." Another peal of bubbling laughter. "But he won't intervene tonight."

And he lunged at me.

I ducked under the descending sweep of steel and kicked over the dressing table. The candle toppled to the floor, igniting the bottom sheet on a mound of faded yellow newspapers. The brittle pages burst instantly into flame.

Taking advantage of the moment, I scrambled through the bookcase door back into the library—with the Fiend right behind me, brandishing his sword. The blade sliced air an inch from my neck as I bent low, closing the fingers of my right hand around an iron fire poker.

"Now, you bastard, this is for Danny!" And, as I straightened, I brought the heavy weapon up in a swift, savage arc, smashing the poker directly across the madman's head.

He screeched like a wounded bird, falling back against one of the antique chairs and dropping the sword to clutch at the bleeding bone-and-gristle ruin of his face.

Then he collapsed with a groan of expelled breath, his loose body spilling along the rug. He lay facedown, unmoving.

I stood over him as a tide of fire spilled into the library from the hidden chamber behind the bookcase.

The entire room was a mass of leaping flame when I walked away from my brother's killer, down the long corridor, across the entry hall, to pause at the outer doorway.

I listened for a long, satisfying moment to the red inferno that was rapidly devouring wood and drapes—and flesh.

"Die, Clown, Die!" I said.

Then I left Wainwright House.

This is the shortest story in the collection, and rates the shortest preface.

I like to deliver surprise endings and "I'll Get Away With It" certainly qualifies.

So be surprised.

I'll Get Away With It

I watch a lot of TV. Old horror movies are my favorites. With Boris Karloff and Bela Lugosi. Where he's a walking dead man, Boris is, with his neck broke and his head all tilted to one side, out to get revenge on the guys who hanged him. Or the one where Bela sucks everybody's blood out and wears a long black cape with a red silk lining. Neato.

There was one I really liked a lot, about this kind of horror hotel where the guy buries people up to their necks in his backyard and they look like cabbage heads sticking up. Then he cuts the heads off. It's a real good one. I've watched it three times on TV.

So I'm home watching an old horror movie when Pop comes in. It's one about the Tower of London (wherever that is) and Boris has got a clubfoot that makes him walk funny and he carries a longhandle ax with a real sharp blade. The movie has kings and royal people in it.

Anyhow, Pop comes in the door looking sour like he always looks at me. "That horror crap you watch is sickening."

"Not to me," I say. "I like it."

"Turn it off," he says.

"No, I like it."

125

"Dammit, are you going to turn that crap off?"

"No."

And he hits me with his fist. Knocks me off the stool I was sitting on in front of the TV and I hit the floor. Blood is on my lip.

He's been hitting me all my life. Ever since I was a little tiny kid Pop's been hitting me. Sometimes he beats me with a belt that has sharp metal stud things on it that hurt and cut my skin. He used to laugh at me when my pants were down for the beating and call me "lard ass" and say I ate too much and that I was a frigging fat pig of a son. *Frigging* is a word Pop likes to use.

All that was when I was real little. I'm a lot bigger now and I'm not fat anymore. I'm skinny. He still makes fun of me. Calls me "Mr. Breadsticks" because my arms are so long and thin. Nothing pleases Pop. Never has. He's always had it in for me.

So, tonight, I decided to kill him.

The idea of him being dead is neato. He belongs dead, like Boris Karloff, the only difference is he won't come back like a zombie to get me. That's just in the movies where dead people do that.

I get up from the floor and walk over to a table that we have near the hall, where Pop keeps a loaded gun. Some kind of shiny automatic, I don't know what kind.

Pop has his back to me turning off the TV when I take out the automatic from the table drawer and shoot him with it. Four or five times I shoot him, I didn't count.

There's plenty of blood because it takes him a while to die. He does a lot of gurgling and gasping and then he doesn't move anymore and it's all over.

I'm glad.

That's when Mom comes home from where she was at

some health club to help her figure. She looks real shocked to see Pop on the floor dead the way he is and says oh God, oh my God, my God, over and over.

I know, right then, I've got to kill her too. No way not to because she'll know I killed Pop and besides she never did anything to help all those times he beat me for nothing. She just walked away and let him beat me.

So I shoot Mom. Another bunch of shots. Automatics have lots of shots in them.

She falls over Pop's body like in some kind of dance and there's more blood and the living room rug in front of the TV is a real mess

I move my stool over and switch the TV back on so I can watch the rest of the horror movie, which is really good. Boris has these mean dark eyes and he looks like he could just eat you up. He cuts people's heads off in the movie. That's his job.

When the movie's over I dial 911 and tell the lady who answers that a terrible, terrible thing has happened at our house, that a robber came in and tried to steal things and Pop tried to stop him and he shot Pop and then he shot Mom after Pop was dead. Now they are both dead on the floor in front of the TV and it's just terrible what happened.

After the phone call I sit down to wait for the people to come. They'll be here soon to deal with Mom and Pop.

Neato.

Everything's cool.

Even if they end up thinking I did it, so what? I'll get away with it. The cops can't do a frigging thing to me. Not really.

What can they do?

I'm only nine years old.

*The story you are about to read exists only because of Joe Lansdale. It's a clone to an earlier story of mine, "The Francis File," (**Best of Whispers**), nearly identical in structure and basic content, although in "Hi, Mom!" all of the interior wording is new.*

Here is how it evolved . . .

In 1989, at the World Fantasy Convention in Seattle, I did a reading of "The Francis File." Joe was in the audience. "Take out the fantasy ending and I'll buy it for my next anthology," he told me.

Sorry, the story had already been sold.

*A month later he phoned. He **had** to have this story. Would I redo it with a new, non-fantasy ending? "But if readers see both stories they'll think I'm stealing from myself."*

"Not," said Joe, "if you write a preface explaining how it happened."

So I sold Joe the alternate version. And I called it "Hi, Mom!"

Joe still hates the fantasy ending in "The Francis File."

There's no fantasy in "Hi, Mom!"

*Me, I like **both** versions.*

Hi, Mom!

Among items found by police in the apartment of William Charles Kelso, 4200 E. Ivy, Hays City, Kansas:

ITEM: A pair of recently severed human hands. Female. Each fingernail lettered in red nail polish.

B-I-L-L-Y (on left hand) K-E-L-S-O (on right hand). Lettering identified as by subject, William Charles Kelso.

ITEM: A baby's plastic rattle, pink. Apparently belonged to subject, W.C.K., when infant.

ITEM: A Sportsman's hunting knife with yellow bone handle, human hair adhering. Bloodstains on blade from victims, various.

ITEM: A photo, undated, of W.C.K. as young boy (five? six?) standing in back yard of unidentified house next to his mother, Mrs. Ella Patrick Kelso. Mother's features (Caucasian) defaced by knife cuts across photo. Word, "SLUT!" written in blue ink by subject at margin of photo, with arrow pointing to Mrs. Kelso.

ITEM: A scrap of what appears to be butcher's wrapping paper, undated. Written (in pencil) on paper by subject:

> I am a void
> I am not part of this planet
> There is no Billy Kelso

ITEM: A snapshot (faded, n.d.) of Mr. and Mrs. Kelso seated on cement steps of apartment house (location unknown) with subject as infant in arms of Ella Kelso. Father is black. Full name: Leonard Edward Kelso. Written across back of snapshot (blue ink) in subject's hand:

> This is only photo I have of my goddam father. The bastard split when I was four. Used to beat up Mom a lot when he was drunk. She's

129

deaf in one ear because of a table fork he stuck in there. I hope he got cancer. Hope it hurt a lot and that he rots.

ITEM: A typed school report sent to Mrs. Kelso from grade school teacher Catherine Vanne in 1966 when subject was eight years old:

> Your son Billy is a very difficult child to control in class. He openly rebels against all forms of discipline. On the playground today he attacked a smaller boy with a wooden bat and had to be physically restrained. Billy is aloof, and has made no friends among his classmates. If his behavior does not show a marked improvement over the remainder of this semester he will be expelled.

Subject added, in blue ink, at bottom of this page:

> Mom whipped me plenty bad for this with her leather belt. Later, I was real dizzy and started spitting blood. Mom says maybe I've got an ulcer.

ITEM: A membership card in an organization known to be on Anti-American list by FBI. Card is marked:

> Cancelled. Non-Caucasian.

ITEM: A human ear. Female. Found in ziplock bag in subject's refrigerator.

ITEM: A poem, undated. Pencil. In subject's adult hand:

Moonlight eating
severed flesh
in dreams
of icy death

ITEM: A loose news clip from the *Daily Register*, Benford, Illinois, dated July 10, 1968:

CAT MYSTERY SOLVED
Local Boy Admits Killing Felines

In response to a neighbor's phone call, local police entered the home of Mrs. Leonard Kelso, 1222 Vincent Avenue, to discover the decomposed bodies of some two dozen cats listed by owners as missing over the past year. The animals were buried in the dirt in one corner of the Kelso basement. They were headless.

Mrs. Kelso's 10-year-old son, William, told police that he was responsible for slaying these animals, but could not remember what he'd done with the heads.

The boy was taken to Juvenile Hall.

ITEM: A child's sketch (by W.C.K.) done when subject was attending grade school in Benford. In colored crayon, sketch shows a row of downtown office buildings with red-and-yellow tongues of flame coming from the windows. At bottom of this sketch, in child's hand:

FIRE IS NICE

ITEM: An untitled story, written in pencil by W.C.K.

(when schoolboy) in blue-lined tablet, n.d.:

> Once upon a time there was a littel boy named Billy who had a Daddy that was called a niger who used to hit his Mom before he went far away to another place. Billy was also called a littel niger but his Mom told him he was white like her so he didn't know which he was and he wanted to run away with a circus and get his face painted all colors like a klown's is.

ITEM: A plastic bag found in subject's bedroom, stuffed with human hair, used as pillow.

ITEM: A copy of the Benford High School Yearbook for 1975. On page 79 is a student graduation photo of subject, with description beneath:

> "Billy." Independent. Quiet. Not one of the crowd. A nut for boxing. (Don't get him sore at you!) Odd sense of humor. Likes small animals. Ambition: "to be an undertaker:" (He's *got* to be kidding!)

ITEM: A private reel-to-reel tape recording:

TAPE BEGINS

Voice of young woman: What *is* this shit? Are you recording us?

Voice of William Charles Kelso: That's right.

Woman: Well shut it the fuck off! I didn't come here to be put on some fucking tape.

Kelso: Watch your mouth. I don't like to hear a lady talk like that.

Woman: And who says I'm a lady? Okay . . . are you going to shut it off or not?

Kelso: No, I'm not.

Woman: Then I'm splitting. Since we didn't do anything I'll just charge you ten bucks. For coming over.

Kelso: You're not leaving.

Woman: The hell I'm not! I don't dig freaks. Get out of my way, damn you!

(SOUNDS OF STRUGGLE)

Kelso: You're never going to leave me again, Ella.

Woman: (terrified) I'm not Ella! . . . who the fuck is Ella?

Kelso: Time to die, slut!

(STRUGGLE INTENSIFIES.
SOUND OF BLOWS.
A HIGH-PITCHED SCREAM.
GASPING. SILENCE.)

TAPE ENDS

ITEM: A pair of initialed white-silk underpants. Initials: E.K. (Thought to have belonged to subject's mother.) Slashed repeatedly with knife.

ITEM: Letter, hand-written, dated November 7, 1984, from ex-convict Alvin P. Stegmeyer to subject (then living in Indianapolis):

> Dear Billy,
>
> Hey, old buddy, how are things? You promised to keep in touch when you left the joint. How come I never hear from you? As for me, just like I told you, I am back in K.C. in the plant, working as a meat packer. Job is okay, and I am back with my girl Nancy and get laid

regular. You getting any? I hope you are, because a guy needs his pussy! (ha, ha) Why not come out to K.C. and visit an old pal? Have you watched one of those 500 Indy races yet? I hear they are great to see with lots of crashes into the wall. (ha, ha) Well I'd better go. Take it easy, buddy, and let me hear from you.

Your friend Al

P S. Still looking for your Mom? As for me, I never want to set eyes on my old lady ever again. She never done nothing good for me. Or for my sis or brothers either, that's for sure. Maybe because you don't have sisters or brothers your Mom treated you better. Anyway I hope you find her.

See you, Al

ITEM: A magazine article, torn from a copy of *Psychology Today*, dated October 3, 1985. Titled: "Portrait of a Compulsive Killer," by Anne Franklin. Following paragraph underlined in red by subject:

With each subsequent murder, this type of maladjusted individual compulsively repeats his ongoing pattern of violence. He is unaware of why he must kill since the elements leading up to his acts are usually deep-rooted in childhood and he has no conscious realization of what motivates him.

He is satisfied only with the death of his latest victim (usually chosen at random). This pattern remains unbroken until he is either apprehended or commits suicide. (Between killings he may experience severe guilt or remorse for his aberrant behavior, but these periods are not constant.)

ITEM: A list, scribbled in subject's hand, on sheet of lined notepaper:

> Kill her dog
> Break into her house
> Kill her
> Get momento (maybe her thumbs???)
> Burn house

ITEM: A scrapbook of news clips (collected by subject) relating to murders ascribed to William Charles Kelso:

> COED FOUND FATALLY STABBED IN UNDERGROUND PARKING LOT

> MOTHER AND BABY SLAIN IN HOME

> TEENAGERS BEATEN TO DEATH ON HIGHWAY

> PATTERN OF KNIFE MURDERS POINT TO SERIAL KILLER

ITEM: A postcard from subject (sent from motel in Jasper, Wyoming) to Kelso's mother in Chicago, dated December 15, 1984. (Card was returned, stamped "Address Unknown"):

> Hi, Mom!
>   Plenty cold this time of year in Wyoming. In

Chicago too I know! The wind sounds like people screaming. How are you? I am pretty good except for the bad dreams that wake me up sometimes at night. You can write me care of the postoffice here in Jasper in case I leave this motel. Working as a frycook at a burger place. I'm doing okay but I need to see you.

> Your son,
> Billy

ITEM: A poem, written on back of a large brown mailing envelope in subject's hand, n.d.:

> Teeth of acid
> tear my flesh.
> Young flowers bleed
> and worms of fire.
> consume me.

ITEM: Final section of a printed transcript from a televised interview with subject. Show, titled "Insights," telecast over KERO-TV, Missoula, Montana during August of 1988. Interviewer: Dean Hawkins.

> *HAWKINS:* . . . and despite the fact that you warned the psychiatrist that you were still a danger to society and could not function outside prison, the parole board nevertheless released you?
>
> *KELSO:* They did, yes. The prisons in this country . . . they're very over-crowded and don't care much who they let out in

the streets. I kept trying to . . . trying to tell them that I wasn't fit to leave . . . that . . . I didn't want to leave.

HAWKINS: Are you telling us you *like* living in a prison environment?

KELSO: No, I'm not really saying that . . . I . . . well, in a way I guess I do . . . like being in prison better than outside where there's . . . no control.

HAWKINS: What is it you're trying to control?

KELSO: Things I do . . . that I don't like doing.

HAWKINS: Then why do them?

KELSO: Because I *have* to. I don't seem to . . . be able to have any choice.

HAWKINS: Just what things are you talking about?

KELSO: (mumbles—not audible) . . . can't say them. I don't want to talk about them. I got put in prison for robbing a store to get some food after I lost a job I had. But I never got caught for . . . for doing what bothers me.

HAWKINS: Are you, as of today, a danger to society?

KELSO: Yes . . . I am. That's true.

HAWKINS: What is it you want to do with your life, Billy?

KELSO: Get it stopped. End it. I just . . . think it's better if I'm dead. That would be better for everybody.

HAWKINS: But what about your family? Don't you have people who care about you?

KELSO: I got no brothers or sisters. Pop left us

when I was real small, and Mom split when I was ten. Said she . . . couldn't handle me anymore . . . and she put me in a home where I ran away. I looked for her but I could never find her. Now I don't care.

HAWKINS: Maybe she's ill and can't contact you. A mother's love is a strong force.

KELSO: Mom never loved me. She used to . . . to beat me with a belt of hers that had a metal buckle that cut me up pretty bad. I got lots of scars on me from that buckle . . . (Pause) I'd get . . . terrible headaches after she beat me. I just couldn't even think straight. That's when I got a cat from the street and . . .

HAWKINS: And what, Billy?

KELSO: I'm not going to talk about that. I needed to find Mom and tell her . . . about how much she hurt me as a kid. But I guess she doesn't care.

HAWKINS: I see. (Long pause) Why did you volunteer to come here today, Billy?

KELSO: To let people know about how these parole boards let you out of prison when you're not ready to be outside. It's a bad thing for them to do . . . very bad.

HAWKINS: We . . . uh . . . certainly thank you for your honesty. There's no doubt that our overcrowded prison system is in severe need of adjustment . . . Thank you for coming here today to tell your story.

KELSO: I didn't tell a lot of it. I left out the . . . the worst parts. I'd really like to be dead now.

NOTE: With regard to the case of William Charles Kelso: Conclusion, computer transcript of signed statement from Ella Patrick Kelso, freely given in presence of Chief of Police Darren Arnwood and police stenographer Philip Eston, at police headquarters, Hays City, Kansas. Dated June 21, 1990:

. . . and when I got here to his apartment I found all this blood. Billy was on the couch in his sweatshirt, drinking a beer and watching TV. There was blood on his hands and all over his pants and shirt and I knew he'd killed somebody else. I'd been reading about him and I knew it was my boy, Billy, doing all these killings.

He was rotten, like his father. Just no damn good, ever. Didn't give me a minute's peace all the time I had him with me. I never wanted to be the mother of some freak kid like he was. I prayed to the Good Lord to deliver me from such a burden. Billy did sick things from the start, and whipping him didn't change him any. Just made him meaner. Maybe it was his mixed blood. I never should have married no black man, that's for sure. One summer Billy set six fires downtown, but nobody knew it was him.

I heard he'd been looking for me a long time, and then I heard he was here in Kansas working in a bakery. So I drove out here to Hays City, to Billy's apartment, and when he looked up real surprised to see me, and said "Hi, Mom!" I shot him. Six times. In the head and chest. With a boy like that you just have to do your duty as a mother. So I did that.

I did my duty.

*When critic Keith Neilson reviewed my collection **Things Beyond Midnight** he stated that "Nolan [often] puts a likable character into a terrible crisis and watches him squirm until a surprising conclusion is reached."*

Well, here's a perfect example. Ray Thornton, my luck-less private detective in this 1930s story, is certainly likable. He becomes involved in a terrible crisis. And the conclusion, I would hope, is surprising.

So join poor Ray in "Silk and Fire" and watch him squirm.

The wrong woman can play hell with a man.

Silk and Fire

She was a walking cliché.

How can I describe her? The kind of face and figure you see featured in shampoo and toothpaste advertisements in the newspapers, in glossy movie magazines like *Photoplay*, and in the calendars hard-working men pin up in their back storerooms, or maybe hide from their wives at home. Perfect hair, perfect eyes, perfect teeth, perfect skin, perfect lips, perfect breasts, perfect legs . . . and a sweet little bum that was beyond perfection.

She'd poured herself into a full-bosomed red silk dress, extra tight across the hips, with red stiletto heels, a skimpy little red feather hat, soft red doeskin gloves, and a red silk purse. Red and hot, like she'd just stepped out of The Ziegfeld Follies of 1938. Her flowing hair was Harlow blonde, and as alive as a star-white flame. She was beaming out a radio message, and I was receiving, loud and clear.

That's how she was that morning—all silk and fire.

Her smile could blind you, it was so dazzling. She moved like a ballet dancer, or maybe more like a jungle cat, kind of gliding across the floor of my office, comfortable, in command, enjoying her female power.

I was bug-eyed, but no doubt she was used to this reaction from the male sex. My jaw agape, sweat beads forming on my upper lip, my eyes wide in delighted shock, I didn't say anything to her.

Couldn't say anything.

She did all the talking at the start, and my first big mistake was in listening to her. But what man could have resisted such a vision? Certainly not me. Not then. Not ever.

Oh, *now,* sure. *Now* I could tell her to go take a flying jump off the Empire State. But now is now, and then was then. And never the twain shall meet.

"My name is Alicia," she said in her perfect warmed-velvet voice, as she took a chair in front of my desk and crossed her perfect legs. Her silk stockings gleamed up at me, caressed by a shaft of sunlight through my office window. "Alicia Luann Sinniger." (Already I liked the "sin" part.)

I nodded, trying to compose myself, trying to look calm and professional—and not having any luck at it. A faint smile told me she didn't mind.

"I need to hire a private detective, Mr. Thornton, and I was given your name. I came right over from my apartment. I live in the Glenwood Garden Estates on Wilshire."

I nodded again, swallowing with difficulty. My throat was dry. My God, but she was gorgeous!

"I assume your fees are reasonable. I'm single, and I live on a rather slim inheritance from my late father, Timothy Baines Sinniger. Perhaps you've heard of him?"

This time I shook my head. No, I hadn't.

"He was a prominent investor. Bought commercial lots in downtown L.A., back before the boom. They're worth plenty these days, even at Depression prices." She sighed. "Unfortunately, my mother died of pneumonia when I was eight, so Pops raised me. I was his only child, and he adored me . . . treated me like a little princess." She smiled, displaying her perfect teeth. "I *should* be a very rich woman today—but, unfortunately, Pops was also a gambler."

"Cards?" I asked.

"No, horses. He lost most of his money, and all of his property, playing long shots across the board. Said it was more exciting when the odds were against him. He didn't know shit about horses."

It was something of a shock to hear her use a four-letter word. She seemed too . . . ethereal . . . too pure for such language. Of course, as I was soon to discover, she was *anything* but pure. But I couldn't see straight back then; my eyes had been blinded by silken fire.

"I hope you're not a gambling man, Mr. Thornton," she said huskily. "Or an alcoholic. My mother was an alcoholic."

"I'm neither," I said. My voice was a trifle shaky, but the words were coming out okay. "I never gamble, and I confine my drinking to a glass of wine at social events." I grinned. "I don't attend many social events."

She sniffed the air. "But you *do* smoke?"

"A pipe, from time to time, but I'm not a regular smoker. Actually, I'm a man of very few vices."

"That's good to know," she said. "I need someone who is entirely reliable."

"Who referred you to me?"

"A man at the bank where I have my account. Robert Cashman."

"Good name for a banker," I said.

"Do you know him? He seemed to suggest that you were a friend."

"I did a job for him last year. Helped him obtain some evidence in a personal situation. I wouldn't call him a friend, but it was nice he gave you my name." I leaned forward and my desk chair creaked. "Just what is it you want to hire me for?"

"Are you like other private detectives?"

"I wouldn't know. What are other private detectives like?"

"Hard and tough. They carry big automatics and drive fast cars. Like James Cagney."

"I don't think Cagney has ever played a private eye," I told her. "He *did* play a G-Man in '35." I leaned forward in my chair trying not to look tough. "As for me, I'm soft and easy. I don't own a gun—and I drive a '36 Dodge that needs work. My clutch keeps slipping."

Somehow she found this amusing; her laugh was deep and throaty. "I've never hired a man with a slipping clutch."

Despite the sheer pleasure I got from drinking in her beauty I felt a tinge of frustration. When would she level with me? Why was she here? I asked if she'd mind getting to the point.

"Well . . ." She pursed her full lips and then quickly licked them with the tip of her tongue. I got a flash about kissing those lips. They'd be warm and smooth and wet and resilient . . . yielding . . . perfect. "I'm not trying to be evasive," she said. "I wanted to find out what kind of man you are."

I shrugged. "I'm just what I appear to be—a reasonably well-dressed private investigator with a reasonably clean office in Santa Monica. And I charge reasonable fees. Satisfied?"

Her face darkened; a shadow invaded the blue of her eyes, deepening their color. "Have any of your cases ever involved murder?"

I hadn't expected such a question.

"No," I said. "I generally do insurance investigation, or prepare evidence for law firms . . . that sort of thing. No murders. That's for those Warner Bros. movie detectives—the ones who are hard and tough and carry big automatics."

She ignored the wisecrack, frowning at me. "The man I've come to see you about is a murderer." She lowered her eyes. "But I'm the only one who knows it."

"Uh-huh. So who did he kill?"

"It started with the cats. When he lived in New Jersey he had seven cats. Then, when he decided to move to California, he took each cat out into the woods behind his house and shot it in the head. One by one . . . all seven."

"That's not murder," I said. "It's a lousy thing to do, but you can't—"

She cut into my words with angry ones of her own. "Then, when he moved out here to Los Angeles with his wife, he killed her pet dog, a cocker spaniel named Sparky. With poison."

"Okay," I nodded. "So this guy is a real scumball—but has he ever killed a human being?"

"Yes," she said flatly.

That stopped me cold. I stared at her. "Who? Who did he kill?"

"His sister, Gracie. Sid—his name is Sidney Marsh—hated Gracie from the time they were little kids. They never got along. When Gracie followed him out here from New Jersey last July, and begged him for enough money to hold her over until she could get a job, he refused to help. Told her he didn't want her in his life, that she should get the hell away." Alicia hesitated, drawing in a long breath. "Gracie died later that same month."

"How?"

"She was struck down on Sunset Boulevard, just after midnight," said Alicia. "There were no witnesses, and the police had no way of tracing the car that killed her. But I know that it was Sid who drove the car. He murdered his sister because she wouldn't stop pestering him for money. He just waited until she was walking back to her hotel from the bus stop, and then he ran her down in the street—killing her in the same cold-blooded way he'd killed Sparky and those seven cats."

"How do you know for sure that Sid Marsh was the hit-and-run driver?"

She began nervously twisting the thin strap of her red silk purse. Her breathing had quickened; this was apparently tough going for her. "I'm close friends with Patrice, Sid's wife. We were roommates in college together, before she moved to New York and met him."

I shrugged. "So . . . what has your friendship to do with the murder?"

"I still visit with Pat. She and I were able to resume our friendship after she talked Sid into moving here to Los Angeles. I was at her house the day after Gracie was killed and I saw a red stain on the front fender of his car. And the fender was dented. Sid had it straightened out and painted that same week. Took it down to Tijuana to have the work done."

"Why haven't you gone to the police?"

"With what? The car has been repaired. The blood is gone. I wasn't an eyewitness when it happened. What could I bring to the police? I have no evidence to give them."

I leaned back in my creaking chair. "What I don't get is how I fit into this. What is it you want me to do?"

"I'm worried about Pat," she said. "Sid beats her. She has bruises and cuts all over her body; he even broke her arm once. And the beatings are getting worse. But she won't do anything about it. She's afraid he'll kill her if she tries anything—and I think he would. He's a prime bastard."

"So what can I do about it?"

"I want you to follow him, find out where he goes and who he sees."

"How will this help your friend?"

"I'm sure he's having an affair with another woman," declared Alicia. "If I can prove it, then show the proof to Pat, maybe then she'll have enough courage to leave him. She just couldn't allow herself to believe me when I told her that he killed Gracie—but the *one* thing Pat will not abide is another woman in Sid's life. I'll take whatever you're able to find to Pat."

"And what if you're wrong? What if he's out bowling, or playing cards with his pals?"

"I'm not wrong. I'm convinced he'll lead you to the other woman. Just follow him. You'll see."

I nodded. "Okay, I'll take the job. I get twenty bucks a day, plus expenses, and I'll need a hundred up front. Nonrefundable. Which means that if the case takes less than five days, I keep the entire deposit."

"Fine," she said. "I knew we could work together." And while she was fishing out five twenty-dollar bills from her purse she gave me a heated look.

A look with a lot of erotic promise in it.

Silk and fire.

That was how it all began. My agreeing to follow Sid Marsh turned out to be the worst mistake of my life.

I was the fly—and I was headed straight for the web.

I'm a good shadow man. I know how to follow somebody—anytime, anywhere—and not get spotted.

I first learned about shadowing people from Dashiell

Hammett. You know, the hotshot writer who published *The Maltese Falcon* and *The Thin Man*. He was a Pinkerton detective before he quit to become a writer, and when he was with the Pinks he earned this rep as an ace shadow man. He worked out four basic rules:

Keep behind the subject.

Never attempt to hide.

Act naturally, no matter the situation.

Never meet the subject's eye.

Hammett claimed that even a clever criminal can be shadowed for weeks without suspecting it. He'd once tailed a forger for three months without arousing suspicion. Hammett taught me that you don't worry about a suspect's face. His carriage, the way he wears clothes, his general outline, his individual mannerisms and physical habits are much more important to a shadow man than faces.

I used to practice on my Mom, when I was a kid. I'd follow her around when she went shopping, and back then I was sure she never spotted me. Now, I'm not so sure. She knew I was into this private operative stuff so maybe she just *pretended* not to see me skulking along behind her. I guess I'll never know; Mom died three years back.

Once I got into the detective game I became an accomplished shadow. I have a natural gift for it. But I'd never followed a murderer, so I was more than a little nervous waiting in my Dodge a half-block up from the home of Sid and Patrice Marsh. Alicia had provided the address: a white two-story Territorial-style in Hollywood. She'd described Marsh as being tall, with a skinny neck and jug ears. And she told me what he drove. A dark green 1937 Packard.

The Packard was parked in the driveway in front of the house when I drove past there late that afternoon. Once I'd spotted his car I parked under a big pepper tree at the far end of the block. The Marsh house was on a cul-de-sac, so he'd have to pass me going anywhere.

I dug out my pipe, fired it up, and waited, puffing away contentedly, thinking about Edward G. Robinson. He smokes a pipe in the movies. A lot of the kids I knew in high school took up smoking cigarettes, but I held out for a pipe. Gives a certain dignity to a man, I always thought. Like Robinson.

An hour crawled by before the green Packard slid past me, driving toward Franklin. A skinny-necked character with jug ears was at the wheel. Who else but Sid Marsh?

He turned left on Franklin, and followed that to Western, with me three car lengths behind him. He turned right down Western, passed Hollywood Boulevard, and turned right again on Carlton. He pulled over, parked, got out, and walked to a modest, one-story, dun-colored frame house, where he keyed open the front door and went inside.

A black Ford coupe was parked in the drive. I eased over to it and looked inside. The registration slip wrapped around the steering wheel bore this Carlton Way address and the owner's name: Lanie Harris.

Ha! The other woman? If so, then this job was a piece of cake. Inside the house Sid Marsh could be in the sack with Miss Harris—or getting there fast.

It was almost dark. The sun had taken a dive toward the ocean and the streetlights were blinking to life.

I waited for full darkness before leaving the car. No one was on the street so I was not observed as I walked along the gravel drive at the left of the house to a rear window that threw a yellow square of light into the darkness. I could see plenty, and there was plenty to see.

Sid Marsh was buckass naked on a narrow bed, pumping away like one of those Long Beach oil derricks. The panting female beneath him just *had* to be Lanie. She had a trim little figure, from what I could see, and a tiny nose which was probably sprinkled with freckles. A genuine redhead, I saw, and all redheads have freckles. The bedside radio was playing Guy Lombardo, sweet and low.

I had my camera with me and took a few choice shots of the action. It was nice of them to leave the light on because I didn't have to use my flash. They were both grunting toward a climax when I walked back to my car.

I congratulated myself. I was smug and self-confident, grateful for the easy hundred I'd earned.

I was also a damn fool.

The pictures turned out fine. Developed them myself. Clear and explicit. Sid Marsh in some very compromising positions with his lady love. Hotcha stuff.

The next morning, when I handed the package over to Alicia at her apartment on Wilshire she was delighted. We were sitting together on a big overstuffed silk sofa and she was literally smacking her lips over the evidence I'd brought her.

"You *did* it, Ray!" she said with a real note of triumph in her voice. (I'd told her to call me Ray. "Mr. Thornton" was just too damned formal.)

"You really think this will cause your friend to leave that creep?"

"I really do," she said, scanning each shot with obvious relish. "They'll drive her nuts!"

It was rough, sitting here next to her, talking about the case, when I felt like grabbing. Body heat seemed to radiate from her, and the rich, sultry smell of her gardenia perfume enveloped me like a dense cloud.

It was early morning, and she was wearing a pale pink satin robe, loosely belted at the waist, over some filmy lace thing that she'd slept in that night. The image of her lying in bed kept popping into my mind . . . her hair tousled . . . her shoulders bare . . . begging me . . .

I stood up abruptly from the sofa.

"What's wrong?" she asked.

"I have to go," I said, not meeting her eyes. "If I don't, something might happen."

"Like what?" There was a teasing lilt to her voice.

"Like my kissing you, for one thing."

I looked into the heated blue of her eyes; her gaze was direct and inviting.

"Hey, you *deserve* a kiss for these snapshots."

She stood up, looping her arms around my neck. The front of her robe had fallen open and I got a good look at those perfect breasts. Crimany!

We kissed. Her lips were as hot as a branding iron; at least they seemed that way, or maybe it was her steamy breath as she pressed her body into mine.

The point is, this wasn't just a kiss, it was the beginning of the most intense sexual experience of my life.

In bed, she was incredible. She took me away from this world, anticipating every desire, matching my intensity with hers. She wove a spell, taking me up and down, up and down, over and over again until, at last, my orgasm was so shattering I almost blacked out. And at last we lay side by side, our bodies immobile and our breathing still labored, like two exhausted sailors after a typhoon.

"Was that good for you?" Alicia finally asked, the blue of her eyes a banked fire.

"Is a 90-pound robin fat?"

She giggled and all her curves rippled. "I think you like sex."

"I think I like *you*."

"Same thing," she said. She rolled away from me on the bed. "You'd better get dressed and leave now. I have things to do."

"Like taking my pictures to Patrice Marsh?"

"Yeah, that's top of the list."

I slipped from the warm, scented bed, hating to leave her. "Call me at the office. Let me know what she says—and when I can see you again."

She reached across the sheet to take my hand. Her fingers were warm and firm. "You'll hear from me soon."

I got dressed and, with great reluctance, left.

Late that afternoon the office phone rang. My heart jumped at the sound. "Thornton," I said.

"It's me."

And it was. Hearing Alicia's voice was like listening to fine music.

"How'd it go?" I asked.

"Not well." A note of regret darkened her tone. "Pat was very upset over the pictures, but instead of getting mad, she got depressed. Said it was all her fault, that if she'd been a better wife Sid would never have taken up with another woman."

"Then she's not going to leave him?"

"Nope. Pat thinks she can lure him back to her. She's going to buy new clothes, have her hair restyled, try some new makeup and perfume." Alicia sighed. "The whole thing's a washout."

"I'm sorry."

"She's even going to tell Sid that she knows about Lanie Harris. Thinks it will bring them closer."

"How will Sid react to that?"

"He won't like it. I said that if she told him what she knows about the Harris woman it would be a big mistake. He'll think she's been spying on him."

"And you can't talk her out of telling him?"

"Not a chance. Pat's a stubborn mule when she sets her mind on something. She was that way in college. No, I was wrong. She just won't listen to me."

"What do you think Sid will do when she tells him?"

"Probably beat the hell out of her," said Alicia. "Or worse."

"Worse? What could be worse?"

"He could kill her." A cold finality in her tone.

"C'mon, you must be stretching it."

"You don't know him, Ray. I do. He's quite capable of killing her. Don't forget what he did to his own sister."

"But the police would—"

"Oh, he'll make it look like an accident. Sid's a very clever fellow. The cops won't be able to lay a finger on him. He'll see to that."

I shifted uncomfortably in my chair. "We should do something."

"I've been thinking exactly that," she agreed. "Can you meet me at four in Hollywood? I'll park a block east of Pat's house."

"Well, sure, but—"

"I'm going in there and take Pat away. I'll have her stay with me at my place. At least until I can talk some sense into her head."

"And you want me along in case Sid gets violent?"

"You got it. You'll be my bodyguard. And bring a gun."

"I don't have one, remember?"

"Then buy one. I'll pay for it. To be on the safe side."

"Guns are never safe."

"Just do it, Ray. For *me* . . . okay?" Her voice had turned sultry again and I could feel myself melting inside. My God, I wanted this woman!

"Okay," I said, "but it's against my principles."

"Which reminds me . . ." Now her voice was husky. "You have very *nice* principles."

The sexual innuendo was plain, and it aroused me. Hell, if purchasing a handgun was all it took to get back between the sheets with her then I'd do it without question. Alicia was a fire running in my blood.

"All right," I said. "I'll have a gun with me when I get out there."

"Can you still make it by four?"

"Sure. Getting the heater won't be that tough. I know a gent I can contact."

"Great! Then I'll see you at four."

And she ended the call.

I drove into downtown L.A. to a pawnshop on Broadway. Some shabby characters ambled the streets, clutching paper-sacked wine bottles. A panhandler approached me as I got out of the car, a rag-haired crone toting a burlap sack stuffed with rotted clothing and yellowed newspapers.

"Hey, mister," she croaked, thrusting out a grimy palm. "Help a starvin' old lady an the good Lord'll bless ya forever!"

She looked like a plucked chicken, and very likely she *was* starving. I gave her a buck. She closed her claw hand around the bill and skittered off. There was a bar two doors down. She darted inside. My dollar would buy several shots of rotgut. Ah, well, maybe she needed it as much as I needed Alicia.

I walked into Eddie Fletcher's place. The air was close and musty and thin bands of sunlight from a slatted window barely penetrated the dim interior.

The store was a jumble of second-rate merchandise typical

of a musty downtown pawnshop. I picked up a fake-gold wristwatch; the band fell off. I was stooping to pick it up when a frog-voiced man behind me said, "Whatcha doin' messin' with that?"

It was Eddie, and when I turned to face him he lit up like a Christmas tree. "Cripes, Ray, it's been a lousy *century* since I've seen ya!" He came over to give me a bear hug. He smelled of sour sweat and nickel cigars.

"I don't get downtown much anymore," I said.

"Want a drink? I got some good hootch in the back."

"I could use some hot coffee," I told him. "Got any?"

"Yeah, I got coffee. Hell, I *always* got coffee."

We walked through a swinging bead curtain into an even mustier room with a chipped cot, a teetering wood table, a dirty washstand, and a leaking toilet. Ed's living quarters. The coffee was simmering in a dented enamel pot atop a rusted stove in one corner. Ed poured me a mug, filling his from a bottle of Wild Turkey.

"Mud in yer eye," he said, taking a deep swig. I took a sip of black coffee so strong it could have revived a corpse, and then we sat down at the oilcloth-covered table.

"You want somethin', an' I got what you want," said Eddie. "Am I right?"

"You're a mind reader, Eddie," I said, grinning at him.

Fletcher looked like an overage pirate—with a frayed leather patch covering his left eye and several teeth missing. His denim shirt was ripped, and stuffed into a pair of ragged work pants that badly needed to see a washtub. He was barefoot and his toenails were dirty.

"What can I do you for?"

"I need a heater. I've got the cash," I said, taking out my wallet.

"You want the untraceable kind?"

"Yeah. Just in case something should go wrong."

"Cost you more."

"Fine."

"Gonna shoot the mayor, are ya? Hell, he's nothin but a goddamn crook! Never trust an Italian, I tellya."

"I don't intend to shoot anybody, but I need the rod today." I stood up. "Show me one."

"Just hold your horses! Sit back down and wait here," he growled. "I'll go fetch what I got."

He shuffled over to a rusted metal cabinet and brought out a large pine box that was missing a hinge. He placed the box on the table, opened it, and shoved it toward me.

"Take yer pick," he said.

Inside the box, set into badly worn black velvet, were three hand weapons: a .45 automatic, a .38 Smith & Wesson Special, and an old-fashioned Colt six-shooter.

"They're all oiled an' loaded," Eddie declared. "Fine stock. Dependable."

"How much for the automatic?" I weighed it in my hand.

He named a price. It was worth maybe half what he asked, but I paid him and slipped the gun into my coat.

"You want more rounds, they're extra," he said, shutting the box.

"No, I'm fine." I stood up again, anxious to get out of the place; I needed to breathe some air that didn't reek of sweat and cigar smoke.

"Ya oughta come down here some Friday night and get into a poker game with me an' the boys . . . Like ole times."

"Yeah, maybe I'll do that," I said, thinking, sure, when pigs fly.

Outside, I saw the old lady again. She started toward me, then realized that she'd already put the squeeze on me. She swung around sharply in the opposite direction and hobbled off.

This was a good place to get away from.

I made a quick stop in Santa Monica for a late lunch. Then, with the loaded .45 in my coat pocket, I took Wilshire all the way into Hollywood. It was a crisp October day and the rolling hills were a rich brown, like burnt toast. There wasn't much traffic, so I made good time, even with my slipping clutch.

It was just four when I met Alicia, right where she said she'd be, a block up from the Marsh house. She was waiting inside her car. She waved when she saw me, got out, and walked back to my Dodge. Her provocative, hip-swinging gait seemed to be a preview of future delights, and I counted myself as one lucky gent.

Actually, my luck was about to run out.

Once she was seated next to me in the Dodge I showed her the .45 automatic. She nodded. "I don't know anything about guns," she said, "but this one looks potent enough."

"If need be, I can wave it at Sid to scare him off," I declared. "Maybe he'll be reasonable and let your friend go with you."

"I wouldn't bet on it," she told me.

"So what's next?"

"Drive down the block and park in front of the house. You stay with the car and keep the motor running."

I grinned. "You make it sound like a 'B' movie. I thought I was supposed to go in with you for backup."

"I hope I won't need you," she said. "If things get out of hand I'll give a yell. Okay?"

I shrugged. "Sure, if that's how you want to play it."

I parked where she told me to, directly in front of the Marsh place, and she went inside. There was a queasy feeling in the pit of my stomach. I had a hunch that things might, indeed, "get out of hand."

And I was right.

First, there was silence from the house. And silence on the street. No other cars were moving. The engine of my Dodge, purring like a big cat under the hood, was the only sound I heard—until the scream.

A woman's scream, piercing, desperate. Alicia or Pat? I couldn't tell. And it didn't matter.

I jumped out of my car and ran for the house. The front door was ajar. I dived inside, the automatic clutched in my right hand.

Alicia was halfway down the stairs, looking as if the Devil himself was after her. Obviously, the scream was hers.

"What happened?"

"Sid!" she gasped, her breath coming in short bursts, her face tight and flushed. "He swore he'd kill us both!" She jerked her head toward the second floor. "Pat's up there with him."

"I'll handle this," I said, quickly mounting the stairs. "You stay here."

"He's got a gun!" she warned me. "Be careful!"

"I'm no hero," I said. "I'll be *very* careful."

My heart was doing a tango inside my chest and my mouth was parched. I could barely swallow. This kind of action was totally alien to me.

I found them in the main bedroom.

Pat was backed against the far wall, next to French doors, which led to an outside deck. She was wild-eyed and shaking. "He . . . he tried to *kill* me!" Her voice was strained and the words were delivered in a terrified half-whisper.

"Where's Marsh?"

"There!" She pointed toward a short inner hallway connecting bedroom and bath. Marsh was on the garnet-colored rug, sprawled on his stomach, unmoving.

"He was . . . going to shoot me," she said brokenly. "I hit him with a chair."

A carved-wood chair from Pat's dressing table lay over-turned on the rug. One of its legs had been splintered.

Marsh groaned softly, beginning to regain his senses.

"He's still got the gun!" wailed Pat. "*Shoot* him!"

"I can't do that. He's only half-conscious. I can handle him without—"

She darted across the room to snatch the .45 from my hand. "If you won't . . . I will!"

She aimed the weapon directly at her husband, triggering it three times, the shots like triple thunderclaps in the room. All three bullets found a home in Sid Marsh.

He wasn't groaning anymore.

"Jesus!" I muttered, staring at the fast-spreading pool of wet crimson staining the rug.

"Here!" She tossed the .45 to me and, instinctively, I caught it in mid-air. "Let's get out. *Now!*"

"But we can't just *leave* him here," I protested.

"Sure we can. Sid won't mind." She was suddenly icy calm, her face an emotionless mask. "Let's go."

I knelt down to check his pulse. Nothing. Marsh was dead.

"Come on," she urged, pulling me up. "Alicia is waiting."

"Let her wait. I'm calling the cops."

She smiled at me. "Go ahead, if that's what you want. Tell them you just murdered Sid Marsh. I'm sure they'll be interested."

I glared at her. "I didn't kill him, *you* did!"

"The shots all came from your gun," she said, her voice like edged steel. "And you're holding it. Your fingerprints are on it."

For the first time, I noticed how she was dressed. As if she were going out shopping: a smart afternoon frock, a little matching hat . . . and gloves. She was wearing *gloves*.

"And besides," she continued, smiling at me. "I'm an eyewitness. I saw everything. I tried to stop you from killing my husband, but I was helpless."

"She's right," said a familiar voice. "You're a killer, Ray."

Alicia was standing in the bedroom doorway. "You shot an unarmed man."

"Unarmed?"

"Sid never owned a gun in his life," said Pat. "Roll him over. See for yourself."

Alicia smiled. "I'd say you're in big trouble, Ray. Big, big trouble."

I've been writing all this from the cell where I'm being held without bail, which the judge refused because the charge is first degree murder. I couldn't raise that much money anyhow. My lawyer, a guy I don't much like, advised me to plead temporary insanity when we go to court.

"The jury probably won't go for it," he told me. "But it's the only chance you've got."

According to the cops and the D.A.'s office, the basic facts are crystal clear:

1. I tried to rape Patrice Marsh in her own bedroom.
2. Her husband came home and attempted to stop me.
3. I shot him to death.

Just like that, one . . . two . . . three. Poor Sid's wife was a horrified witness to this brutal killing. And according to a signed and sworn statement, Alicia Sinniger had driven over there that day to visit her friend. She was stunned to encounter me upstairs, the gun still in my hand, Sid Marsh dead on the floor. Patrice was hysterical with shock and grief, so Alicia had phoned the police after I left. Pat's afternoon frock was torn where I had pawed at her in my lust-crazed rape attempt.

Naturally, as expected, I denied everything, swearing that

Pat had shot her husband with my gun. Except that only my prints were on it. I told the cops she'd been wearing gloves, but they never found any. Just my fingerprints on the murder weapon.

I also brought up the fact of motive: Pat had one. Her husband had been brutally beating her over a long period of time.

Ridiculous, Pat had countered. "Sid loved me deeply," she told the police, tears running down her cheeks. "He was a very gentle, caring man. He'd never lay a hand on me. Never!"

She went on to claim that I'd made up a "crazy story" to try and cover my attempted rape and the murder of her beloved husband. She'd never forget Sid's courage, coming to her rescue bare-handed against a gun-wielding rapist-killer.

It was a great job of acting. Academy Award all the way.

A court-appointed doctor examined Pat's body minutely, head-to-toe. No evidence of beatings. Not a mark. Not the tiniest evidence of fracture, past or present.

Obviously, according to the police, this grief-stricken widow was telling the truth.

Newspapers headlined the case, branding me as a "vicious murderer" whose story of innocence was laughable. They found a grim, unsmiling photo of me (God knows where) and darkened the area around my eyes before they printed it. I looked like Jack the Ripper.

The *Times* ran a photo interview with a neighbor of mine, Ed Morgan, who described me as "moody and reclusive." Morgan went on to say that he had always felt there was something "kind of spooky" about the way I talked, and that he knew for a fact that I enjoyed reading "dirty books."

Actually, I've never said more than hello to the man, and I never knew his name until I read it in the paper.

The *Times* also reported that the grieving widow would receive a substantial amount of life insurance, thanks to her husband's prudent foresight in taking out a number of hefty policies on his own life. Not that the money could make up for the crippling loss of her husband, of course, but it might help ease her pain and allow her to begin life once again.

I'd been a pawn in this game from the moment Alicia had walked into my office. I'd played right into her hands (and her bed). Everything she'd said to me had been—lies. Sure, Gracie Marsh *had* followed her brother out to California, but Sid hadn't run her down on the street. That, I was certain, was Alicia's doing; it was surely *her* car that had killed Gracie, not Sid's. She had hoped that Pat would blame Sid for killing his sister and leave him—but that didn't happen. Pat had no money of her own; she was financially dependent on Marsh and wasn't about to give up what she had.

Then Alicia and Pat put their heads together and came up with the bright idea of setting up someone as Sid's killer so they could share the insurance money. I was the someone they picked. A lust-happy private investigator who'd go for Alicia like a cat goes for fresh cream.

What a prime sap I'd been!

More lies to me about wife beating. And as for Sid's affair with Lanie Harris—hell, Pat knew all about that and didn't care. She refused to have relations with him. He wasn't what she was interested in.

I found out about that when Alicia came to visit me, Pat Marsh with her.

"Everything was so easy," Alicia told me, looking gorgeous in her tight red silk dress, the same dress she'd worn that first day in my office. "There was only one problem—having to go to bed with you." She grimaced. "That made me sick."

"Yeah," Pat nodded. "Poor Alicia."

They told me they're thinking about moving to Hawaii. Or maybe France. Since college, they said, they've both loved Paris. So *sophisticated* there, they giggled.

They left the jail together, hand-in-hand. Two very good friends.

My trial starts next month.

I call this one a fractured fairy tale, dealing as it does with several of the legendary characters we all grew up with, yet presented here in a new perspective. Is it a crime story? Of course. Snow White is most certainly guilty of murder.

I've always yearned to try my hand at a genuine fairy tale, and found a pleasant satisfaction in conjuring up "Once Upon a Time . . ."

Be prepared to encounter some very old friends in a very new environment.

Disney it ain't.

Once Upon A Time . . .

My name is Snow White and I'm writing this from my house in the woods. Of course, you won't be able to read these words because after you meet me you'll be dead. Guess I'm just a silly goose for putting all this on paper, but it's a way to pass the time while I'm waiting for you.

If I explain, very carefully, why I have to kill you, then maybe somebody else will come along, after we're both gone, and read this and say, "Golly, Snow White wasn't such a bad person. She just did what she had to do. It was Old Meg's fault, not hers—from the world beyond the meadow."

Whoops! I'm getting ahead of myself. Can't talk about another world until I explain what I'm doing in this one. First things first. I'm trying to be very organized about what I have to tell you. The Seven Dwarfs are organized—as a *group,* that is. Individually, they wouldn't impress you. But I don't want to write about them. That's way off my subject.

If I ramble from time to time, hey, I'm no writer. Never

tried to tell a story before in all my days. So bear with me, huh. Give me some goddam slack. That's an Earth expression, from your world, this one I'm in right now. I read it in one of your magazines. People who've come here, to my home in the woods, bring all kinds of things. Food. Toys. Sun hats. Sleeping bags. Tents. Fishing poles. And magazines. Even a book. I tried to read it but it didn't make much sense. About cowboys in something called The Old West. Whatever that is. I figure a cowboy is half-cow and half-boy, and that I can understand. Like our centaurs. I put down the book at the end of the first chapter. Anyhow, one of you came with a magazine that had a man saying, "For Christ's sake, give me some goddam slack!" And the woman was described as being "plenty pissed." I was able to figure it out, but I don't know who Christ is. Doesn't matter. There's a lot about your world I don't know.

Maybe I should tell you about my house and the ones I live with here in the woods. I built the house myself, mostly using my teeth. I have very strong, sharp teeth. They can bite right thorough wood, real easy. I made the house out of trees, with a nice grass roof. I bit in holes for windows so I could look out to see who's coming. Maybe I'll see *you* from one of the holes!

I live here with Ben. He's a unicorn, all muddy-brown-reddish colored. And with Angelbird, who is all white with big wings and an orange beak. (There's another bird who comes to visit, and likes to drink from the stream next to our house, but she can't talk the way Angelbird can.) Then I have Irma and Willie who are kind of grumpy. They look a little like your lizards with lizardy tails, but they're actually snarbs. That's S-N-A-R-B. Of course, you never heard of snarbs because they're from *my* world. When Old Meg—and I'll get to her in a minute—sent me here to your world she sent along Ben and Angelbird and the two snarbs to make sure I had some company. At least, that's what Meg told me. But I know the real reason. The *real* reason is they're supposed to keep an eye on me and make sure I don't go running off somewhere. As soon as I finish doing what I have to do here on Earth they'll disappear—Poof!—and I'll be able to—

Whoa! (That's what the book said they say to horses in "The Old West" from the first chapter.) There I go again, getting ahead of myself with what I want to tell you.

As for running off, where would I run, looking the way I do? Nine feet tall with a big bulgy green eye in the middle of my forehead and with a mouth full of real sharp teeth and four hairy arms that drag on the ground when I walk. In this world of yours, if I ever left the woods, I'd be locked up in a cage like some kind of terrible beast. Yet, all the time, here I am, Snow White, beautiful and slender and waiting for Prince Charming. Well, I *was*. But not anymore. Not now. Oh, no, now I'm big and ugly. You can blame Old Meg for that. She made me look this way.

Maybe I'd better tell you about her. Old Meg lives in a thatch hut deep in the forest and she eats live rats and hates me. Always has. Once she offered me a poison apple, but I was smart enough to say no thanks. It looked delicious, all ripe and plump and shiny, but I knew I shouldn't bite into it, and I didn't. That made her mad. She even stomped on her hat, which gave me the giggles. Then she flew off on her broom.

She's a real witch, all right, and you wouldn't mistake her for anything else. Hook nose with a big wart on the end of it. Pointy chin. Red-glowing eyes. Wears a tattered smelly black dress and black slippers with curled-up toes. Long fingers with rotty nails on them, like claws. And she loves to cackle.

So that's Old Meg.

As I said, she's never liked me. You know, the mean old

witch who hates Snow White because of her beauty. And I am beautiful. Was beautiful, that is. Inside, I still feel beautiful, and I'll be again once I finish what I have to do here in your world. (And I'm depending on you to get the job done!)

Well, let me tell you how I got here, so you'll be clear on things. It started when I turned down the apple. The next morning, when I was in front of my mirror brushing my lovely hair (100 strokes, never less!) Old Meg made a broom-landing outside my little cabin. Stormed in, glaring. Said she was going to put a spell on me as punishment for refusing her apple.

She took me to her smarmy hut in the forest where she had this big iron pot boiling in front of the fireplace. Cackling, she poured in some stinky powder, some snake's entrails, some crocodile tail, a toad's liver, and lots of other awful items and stirred them all up and then dipped a cup into the pot and swallowed what was in the cup. Eck! It *had* to taste foul, but being a witch, this gave her the power to cast her spell. I recall her exact chant:

> Rigga do and rigga dee,
> Thy body will no longer be!
>
> Agga dee and agga day,
> Snow White vanishes away!
>
> Igga op and igga yee,
> To Earth I herewith banish thee!

Which is when I turned into this one-eyed ape creature and ended up here in the woods.

Before I left, Old Meg gave me a Sheet of Basic Instructions, telling me what I'd have to do in order to regain my true body and return to my world. On the sheet are a list of things I have to get in order to break the spell. Different things. All under the heading: FEMALE (Human).

All right, I know you're confused. So let me tell you the whole story in the proper sequence. I just wanted you to know about Old Meg.

Odd thing: I used to worry about Prince Charming finding me. Kept looking for him to show up on his big white horse and ride off with me as his blushing bride. But now I have a lot more serious things to worry about because Old Meg hasn't made it easy for me to break this spell. For instance, there's a time limit. If I don't get all the things on the list within thirty Earth days then I'll be stuck here forever on your world in this ugly one-eyed ape body.

Thirty days. That's all she gave me.

Angelbird says I'll never make it. Ben is more open-minded. The two snarbs won't even talk to me. They just sit around on the rocks eating red berries and getting into arguments with each other. (I'm glad Meg didn't turn me into a snarb!)

"Why *me*, Angelbird?" I ask.

"It's obvious," she says, ruffling her feathers. "Meg is jealous of you. The old 'mirror, mirror on the wall' routine. She can do a lot with her spells, but she can't make herself beautiful. So she made you uglier than she is. And that's going some."

"Angel's right," nodded Ben. "But just hang in there, Snow. You're getting the stuff on her list."

"But I'm running out of time," I say.

"At first, I didn't think you'd make it," Ben admits. "I was wrong." He taps me on the shoulder with his horn. "I'm proud of you, Snow."

That cheered me. Feels good to have a unicorn backing

you up. I didn't think I would, but I truly like Ben. He's turned into a real pal.

To get here, you take I-50 all the way to the Tuskaroot Turnoff and then go left on Stanhope Road for about ten miles into the woods and here I am at my tree-house, waiting.

So far I've been very fortunate in having people drop by. First it was the Rickmans, who were looking for a quiet place in the woods to pitch their tent. A honeymoon situation.

I bit off her **right leg** and then had the snarbs dispose of the two honeymooners. A good start!

Then, about a week later, the girl runner shows up. She was training for some cross-country race and her name was Norma. Got her left arm. Angelbird buried her. (Used her beak to do the digging.)

Next came a long-time-married couple, Grace and Harley Gibbs. On vacation. Looking for a nice spot to have a picnic. They thought my house was a wonderful structure. That was Harley's phrase: "My goodness! What a wonderful structure."

When they saw *me,* however, they didn't think I was so wonderful. Especially when I bit Mrs. Gibbs in half to get her torso.

Young kid on a bicycle shows up two days later. Teenager named Sally. Outdoor type, all tan and supple. I bit off her right arm—and felt I was making some real progress. Ben ran her through with his horn and we cremated her. Gets cold at night here in the woods.

Then I was lucky again. A Girl Scout who'd wandered away from her troop and was lost in the woods. Got her left leg. One quick, clean bite. Toes and all. She's buried by the stream, next to the Gibbes. The snarbs wanted to eat her, but I said that was disgusting. They grumped around for a whole day over that.

Things seemed to be going my way. I was in a really good mood, kidding around with Angelbird and teasing Ben (pulling his tail) when along comes the Sutter family. Bob and Beth and little Jane, who was nine.

Jane wasn't afraid of me, which was nice. She said I looked like something out of one of the fairy tales in her books, which is when I found out that on Earth fairy tales are *not* true! I was astonished.

She told me about Little Red Riding Hood and Cinderella and Rapunzel with her long golden hair and Jack and the Beanstalk. Of course I know all of them personally. In *my* world they're all quite real, like I am. We take dragons and giants and wizards very seriously. If we didn't, they might eat us up!

In that one talk little Jane gave me a whole new insight into what Earth is like.

Naturally, she was no good to me. Female, sure, but too young to bite into. So I had the snarbs deal with her and Bob while I took Beth inside and bit off her left leg. Chomp! Right down to the toes.

And we had another warm fire that night.

Hey, maybe by Earth standards this is upsetting you. Telling about these body parts I'm biting off the females who come by my house. But they're all on Meg's list: two arms, three legs, one torso. Et cetera. If I miss getting any one of them then I'll never be rid of the spell.

I admit I'm a little worried now. A *lot* worried, really. Because twenty-nine-and-a-half days have gone by and I still need the last item on my list. In less than twelve hours the time will be up and I'll never get home.

Never.

Oh, great! I SEE you! Headed this way—straight for my

tree-house. Here you come. Hooray!

It's all over now. You're dead and buried and I'll soon be on my way to the meadow to meet Old Meg and she'll be forced to take me back home. Where I'll be Snow White again, all young and lithe and beautiful. Meg's going to be really surprised that I got all the things on her list in time to meet the deadline, but she's got to play fair, by witch-spell rules. Angelbird and Ben and the two grumpy snarbs have already vanished, so that's a step in the right direction. (Though, like I thought, I'll miss Ben.)

You saved me. When you arrived on your shiny motorcycle I was about ready to give up and just accept having a bulgy green eye and four arms.

But there you were. In a metal-studded leather jacket with "Hell's Bikers" stitched on the back, and boots, and a big black helmet with orange stripes on it. You didn't see any of us around and you were hungry so you went inside my house to look for food. Which is when I jumped on you and got the final item on my list: "One female head, with neck."

This all would have gone *much* faster except that, under the rules of the spell, I could only keep what I get on my first bite. One major body part per female. And since I needed *two* arms and *three* legs and a torso and a head-and-neck combination to complete the list it was really rather difficult. Old Meg figured I'd never get them all in thirty days, one at a time the way I had to do it. But I proved her wrong.

Hooray for me!

Well, that's my story. As I wrote, right at the start, with you dead you won't be reading these words, but that's okay. Maybe somebody else will. I hope they understand that I'm really a good person. I did only what I *had* to do. I really didn't have any choice.

I feel happy now. I met the deadline.

It was actually kind of fun.

Got to go. Old Meg's waiting.

And I bet she's going to be . . . plenty pissed!

The ghost of Charles Beaumont haunts the pages of this story.

Chuck was my best, my dearest friend for more than ten years. We edited three books together, plotted Mickey Mouse comics for the Disney people, wrote a children's book on racing, and collaborated on television scripts. However, when it came to prose fiction, we went our separate ways— until Chuck got the idea for "Down the Long Night" and invited me in. We plotted it together and co-wrote a rough draft. Then Chuck got a TV assignment, ran off to write it, and I was left with our pages.

What you are about to read is my final version. Most of the writing is mine, but some Beaumont sections remain in the narrative. The plot, of course, is pure collaboration.

I've always been fond of this story. Rereading it, Chuck Beaumont comes alive for me again. His death at 38 (as a very early victim of Alzheimers) was tragic and senseless. I'll always miss his raw energy, his enthusiasm, his keen mind and bright talent.

This one, ole buddy, is for you.

Down the Long Night

The ocean fog closed in, suddenly, like a big gray fist, and Alan Cole stopped remembering. Swearing under his breath, he jabbed the wiper button on the Lincoln's dash, and brought the big car down from fifty to thirty-five. Still dangerous. You couldn't see more than a few yards ahead in this soup. But he said the hell with it and kept the Lincoln at thirty-five because he wanted this mess over in a hurry, because he wanted to hold Jessica in his arms again before the night was done.

Above the damp Santa Monica pavements, looped tubes of neon glowed coldly, like colored seaweed; but there were no other cars. Cole shot through a blinking amber eye.

Actually, he thought, I should have turned him down flat. I should have said, Look, Paul, last week you ripped it. Period. So I don't give a good god damn *what* kind of trouble you're in.

But then he heard Paul Bowers's anxious voice again, hard and metallic: *"I've got to see you, Alan."* And he knew that, despite everything—even the way the guy had been acting since Jess had given him the shoulder—he did care. Why?

Nearing Ocean Pier, he thought about the telephone call, attempted to form an attitude. What would he say? For Godsake, how do you talk to a man you've called a loser and a phony and a coddled neurotic?

It had come just after lunch. Cecile couldn't say why she'd put it through against his instructions, except to remark that it sounded important. Of course it had to be Paul. After that screwball telegram from San Francisco, which didn't even start to make sense, Alan had been expecting the call. A big play to get in as a 'friend of the family', no doubt. A well thought out pitch on how sorry he was that he'd blown his stack and, needless to say, he wished them both the best of luck, and would they please forgive him—maybe even invite him to the wedding?

Except it didn't turn out that way . . .

Cole punched loose a cigarette, lit it, and went over the conversation for the umpteenth time, searching for clues.

"I've got to see you, Alan."

"No go. They're shooting this scene tomorrow, and I can't—"

"Alan, listen—I'm in trouble. I need your help."

"Like hell. You don't need anybody's help—unquote."

"Wait—Look, I know I said a lot of stupid things last week. But if our friendship ever meant anything to you, for the love of God listen!"

"Paul, I said I'm busy. I meant it. Let me give you a ring tomorrow."

"Tomorrow is too late." The pleading voice had seemed to crawl from the receiver. A pause. Then: *"The police are after me."*

"You're kidding."

"I swear it! Meet me at the pier when you get off work. Crazyville, the funhouse—you know. And don't laugh. It's the only safe place. I'll be waiting for you, Alan. Don't fail me. It may mean my life . . ."

And then the sharp click as Paul had hung up. Damn him, and damn the day they ever met!

Still, Cole thought, unaware that the Lincoln was wavering on the wrong side of the double white lines, still—it was through Paul that he'd met Jessica. They were engaged then. At least, that's what Paul thought; the poor guy couldn't see how bad he was for the girl. She had been impressed with him, at first. Then, like everyone else, she became disenchanted. And, like everyone else, she had a hell of a time pulling loose.

Was it *my* fault, Cole demanded of himself, that the two of us hit it off so well? I didn't take Jess away from Paul. He'd lost her a long time ago.

He spotted a parking place and nosed the car in, cut the engine, sat a moment, quietly, then opened the door.

Chill air went into his throat; it tasted of brine and heavy salt and fathoms. As he locked the automobile, turned and started to walk down the deserted street, Cole remembered how he had always hated this cold, which had nothing of winter in it; and how Bowers had always loved it. As usual, they disagreed. Over the years their likes and dislikes had seldom coincided. Bowers the social lion, the studied Bohemian—to all outward appearances sophisticated and intellectual; and Cole the recluse, the quiet one, the guy over there in the corner. How, Alan wondered, could two such people ever have formed a strong friendship? And was it really that?

Up ahead, the pier stretched, fog-draped and empty. Only the frozen spokes of the ferris wheel and the rotting wooden lacework of the Hi-Boy rose above the pressing blanket of gray.

Alan moved down Marine Street toward the pier, watching his image ripple and flow past streaked shop windows.

What was it with Paul, anyway? What the devil had he done? Robbed someone—no, that was hard to take, not Bowers's long suit. Or—

He passed a window filled with photographs of wild-eyed matted men in silk trunks. Lord Perkins; The Boston Bull; The Strangler.

—murder?

No.

Another window promised salvation to the penitent, damnation to the wicked.

Hotels, shops, missions—all empty and silent. As they had been a million winters ago, when he and Bowers and Jess had walked this street the last time.

Where are the people? He had wondered then. He wondered it now.

Maybe there aren't any people. You never see them moving behind glass. Maybe—

Alan shook his head. Ease off. You're just nervous. Paul's in trouble of some kind, so you're nervous. This place is nothing more than an amusement park, shut down, closed for the season; and that's all. So knock it off, Cole. You're a big boy now.

Yet, Alan felt a slow fear building in him—an uneasiness. With every step, years were peeling away, stripping off in layers. A few moments ago he was Alan Cole, thirty years old, a moderately successful screen writer and not anxious to be anything else. Now . . .

Marine Street flowed into the wide concrete length of Promenade. Alan hurried across, listening to the thin cries of circling gulls on the lonely night beach.

Taking a final drag on his cigarette, he ground it underheel and turned into the amusement park.

Again the sense of something amiss. Partly Paul and also, this place. As if only a moment before, every stand had been open, every ride spinning and whirling and rolling in colored movements, the walk itself alive with people. And as if magic fingers had been snapped, causing all the people and the movement to vanish instantly.

Passing the roller coaster, Alan could almost hear the chant of the bored, slick-haired ticket seller: *"The Hi-Boy! The Hi-Boy! Don't miss it, folks! It's safe! It's exciting! The Thrill of a Life-Time!"*

He glanced at the sheeted train of wooden cars, waiting in coiled silence on their tracks, and hurried past.

His stomach felt light. Dizziness had returned with memories. ("Jess, I'd like you to meet an old buddy of mine, Alan Cole. Alan, this is my gal, Jessica Randall. Isn't she a doll?") He quickened his step past the closed concessions, endless rows of shabby canvas curtains; past the rifle range and the Whirlagig and the Caterpillar; past the arcade where dreams cost a penny.

A hundred yards ahead, on the tip of the pier, he could see the fog-buried angles of Crazyville.

Paul would be waiting there. And it would all be over soon.

He'd see to that, by God.

The ticket booth was a gigantic smiling head. Within its mouth, between the plaster teeth, a sign read: CLOSED.

Alan paused at the wicket gate and glanced back along the walkway. It was empty.

He vaulted the gate and peered across the yard. A tiny, twisting path marked LOONEY STREET horseshoed around mad wooden building fronts.

Gravity seemed missing here; it was a force that belonged entirely to the outside world. The houses convoluted above the cobbled walk, gables and roofs and walls leaning at impossible angles, one upon the other.

Alan cupped his hands about his mouth. Softly, he called: "Paul."

No answer.

He swore. He hadn't changed; not a bit. This idiot place was supposed to make you dizzy, so—he was dizzy.

And where the hell was Paul?

He moved toward the bat-wing doors, which opened to the black maze of damp tunnels. Beyond this point lay a man-made night so intense and so impenetrable that, once inside, you could no longer imagine day.

"Paul?"

He hesitated, glanced up. A ragged, toothless crone sagged drunkenly from a second-story window. Her throat had been carefully sawcut; her eyes protruded in dumb disbelief.

Bloodied faces peeped from every window, each with a

name and a history. Paul had once claimed that they were his only friends, these plaster nightmares, the only ones who truly understood him.

Standing in the silent yard, Alan felt the familiar horror of the Funhouse engulfing him again. The death-figures seemed to writhe just beyond the perimeter of his vision: he could almost *hear* their frozen cries.

He drew a deep breath, pushed open the doors, and hesitated there, divided squarely between the interior shadows and the solid reality of the outside.

"Paul—you in here?"

Like a huge sounding box, the wooden tunnels bounced the words along, echoing, finally lost.

Then: "Alan?"

"Yeah!" He wiped perspiration from his palms. "Come on out."

A pause. "I can't." The voice was faint.

"What do you mean, you can't?"

"Too dangerous. I might be seen."

"There's nobody around for miles."

"I—can't afford to take the chance."

"All right, all right. God! Where are you?"

"Just follow the tunnel. First room."

"All right, but—this better be *good*."

Alan stepped into the long night of the tunnels; into a colored blackness that danced before his eyes in a million tiny specks of light. The walls, damp and slippery beneath his groping hands, smelled of the sea; the odor of soaked and rotting wood seeped up from the floor. Far below, hidden waters sloshed against tired pilings.

The walls began to narrow as he moved forward. The ceiling lowered gradually. He was forced to crouch, turn sideways.

The walls ended.

Alan extended cautious hands, encountered nothingness. "Okay, so I'm out of the first tunnel. What now?"

"You're fine." The voice was much closer. "Keep coming."

"I can't see a damn thing."

Alan remembered his lighter, got it out, thumbed the wheel. It sparked feebly, failed to ignite. Another spin. A tiny guttering flame this time.

He shielded it with his left hand and peered ahead. A cleated platform led upward, He slid his feet over the cleats and reached a wide opening.

"In here, Alan."

The light flickered. "Well, turn on a flashlight or something, will you! I'm going to fall flat on my ass."

Of course, he realized, Paul must know this place as a blind man knows his own bedroom. Always running out here to "think." Or to bang quail. Or—what?

Alan advanced carefully, tapping. A heavy object brushed his shoulder; he hissed, leaping back. The lighter clattered to the plank flooring and winked out.

Total darkness.

"Paul?"

"Over here."

"Over *where?* What am I, a goddamn cat or something?" There was a scrabbling, a fast padding, "Look, buddy, this routine is getting old at a rapid clip. In fact, the hell with the whole thing. I'm getting out of here."

He patted his handkerchief pocket, removed a matchfolder. He struck one.

The object that had brushed against him was, he saw, a body swinging from a thick rope.

No—not a body. By adjusting his eyes to the feeble glow, Alan saw that it was a scarecrow. One of many. The room seemed filled with hanging straw corpses, all revolving in submarine slowness on their corded lengths of hemp. Scarecrows . . . papier maché trees . . . Now he remembered the room. Horse Thief Hall, or something like that.

The flame bit into his finger.

Blackness.

He lit another match, dropped it, tore the last one out savagely. "Okay, kid, you wanted to talk—here I am."

Silence.

He swung the match in a slow arc above his head, knowing, suddenly, that it was useless, knowing that Paul Bowers's entire phone conversation had been another fake. The sincerity and the pleading and the desperation: all fake. Part of a final, elaborate practical joke. Paul didn't need help; what he needed was a long overdue kick in the teeth!

"Fun's over, Cole catches on!" he called.

Silence.

The third match burned out. Alan turned to retrace his steps, thinking about Jessica's probable reaction to a stunt like this. Maybe he shouldn't tell her. The less said about Paul in her presence, the better.

It takes a certain talent, he thought bitterly; a certain definite talent to be a perpetual fall-guy. Drop the hook, I'll bite!

He'd almost reached the doorway when four naked green bulbs, one in each corner of the room, bloomed into silent life.

Alan blinked, the pale glow burning into his eyes. He scrubbed at them, realizing, vaguely, that Paul had found the central control box and activated a switch.

The swinging scarecrows came into focus. Alan's fist knotted. His head jerked about the room. "Listen!" he shouted, "I'm going to walk back out of here, Paul. Don't try anything cute. Because if you do I swear I'll break your damn neck. Is that clear?"

He started for the opening. Another scarecrow bumped against his shoulder. He wheeled, buried his fingers in the mouldered straw, and pulled, furiously. The figure tore loose at the neck, collapsed to the floor with a wet, pulpy sound.

Soft laughter from the tunnels.

He was about to push his way through the hanging figures when he paused.

Everything inside him paused.

Sensation became thought: *Scarecrows are made of straw.* And the object that had just touched him was *solid!*

Alan turned, and jammed a fist against his mouth.

Hanging there, swaying amid the rotting scarecrows, was Jessica Randall.

For a long moment, Alan could not move. His body was incapable of movement, every muscle locked tight.

His mind tried to reject what his eyes saw.

She was naked. And cold. Her flesh, once warm and vibrant, carried now an icy chill; and her eyes, though unseeing, were open.

Her sheer silk stockings had been knotted about her throat and around a ceiling beam, and supported her slight weight easily.

"Jess!"

Alan put a trembling hand to the girl's breast, and then he knew she was dead.

Jess was dead. And Paul had killed her. He knew that, too. Because she had fallen in love with someone else. Paul had done this, just as he'd promised in that crazy speech he'd delivered to them. They hadn't believed him, or taken him seriously, because Paul Bowers had always been a lot of talk, a thin red-faced clown full of empty promises and emptier threats. And they'd been wrong.

Alan saw Jess's clothes, her red blouse and white skirt, her undergarments, her black leather ballet-shoes—all folded and placed neatly in a corner on the floor. And he knew a hate and a fear, then, that he had never dreamed of.

Run! He thought. Try to stay calm and get out of this place. He wants you to panic. Don't panic. Just get out, quickly—then wait and get him.

He pulled a shutter in his mind that closed off the reality of Jess and what had happened to her. Out, the same way, he thought; but it wasn't so easy. He'd turned so many times that he had lost all sense of direction. Three separate doorways opened on the room of scarecrows and only one of them led back to the first tunnel: the others were phony. And he couldn't be sure which was which.

He'd taken a single step forward, aware now that the laughter was mechanical, not human, issuing from the cracked lips of a plaster fat man, when the ceiling lights blacked out again. Paul was still at the switch and that meant he had little time. Hurriedly, he knelt on the plank flooring and groped for the fallen lighter. Without luck.

Okay, Cole, so you move in the dark—but by God you move!

He touched one wall of the room. He moved along, tapping the rough wood: he would have to try one of the doorways and hope it was the right one.

He thought of Bowers, at home in the darkness, gliding through the looping maze of passageways like a swift fish in green waters, perfectly at ease, perfectly in command.

The funhouse was Paul's world.

Abruptly the wall ended, but not in emptiness. He'd fumbled himself into a corner. A corner—without knowing exactly why, he reached up and touched a light bulb. It was still warm. He unscrewed it in quick short motions and dropped it

183

into his pocket. Then he followed the next wall and reached one of the doors.

Careful to walk slowly, he entered the tunnel. And walked head-on into a wall. Wood on all three sides.

Alan groaned softly, his throat went dry. He tried to swallow and couldn't.

All right, you missed. Now turn around and go back to the next one. Move, damn you, move!

He re-entered the still black room and groped numbly along to the second doorway. At least this one would lead somewhere. Alan stepped out onto the cleated platform.

This must be it! It seemed to possess the same dank odor, the same narrow twistings . . .

He pressed forward.

A buzzing, a whirr of turning machinery, and the blackness blazed into light. Far off, the laughter again. Within a niche in the wall directly to Alan's right, a huge gorilla raised its fists, swiveled its savage head back and forth, snarling.

"You son of a bitch, Bowers! I'll kill you."

The apparition faded behind him. He was running now, knowing that this tunnel led deeper into the funhouse. Toward Paul's voice?

Six explosions, deafening, somewhere in the dark. Gunshots. Paul had a gun. But why waste bullets?

To let you know he's armed. To let you know he's waiting . . .

Alan ran on, constantly aware that in order to get Bowers, he would have to get into the open, into his world. He stumbled, barking his knuckles on trick partitions, pushed himself forward, his face sweatsoaked, legs weak and trembling.

A dragon sprang into colored life. It lay on painted rocks, a fat reptilian creature, its green-scaled head nodding, forked tongues licking in and out.

Sudden shrill gusts of wind hissed up from the floor.

And the infernal laughter, mocking him, following him wherever he went—

He ran on, crouching, sometimes on hands and knees, blundering forward, knowing, even as he ran, that he was close to death. A bullet or a knife would meet him in the darkness; and he wouldn't have a chance.

Then he saw light—faint, but only moments away. Only a few more steps!

The floor dropped from beneath him. Alan felt himself plunging downward; he thrashed his arms, clutched at shadows and blackness.

The trap-door closed.

The room was full of people. Frightened, angry, staring people, all seated at the bottom of a long slide.

A memory clicked into place for Alan Cole. The Mirror Room where you spend an hour, alone, trying to find your way out.

He licked his dry lips and wiped the perspiration from his hands.

He listened. Footsteps.

You're unarmed. Move!

Jerkily, he thrust himself into the corridors of glass. He saw his image reflected in a thousand bright distortions as he slammed through the maze, bumping; cursing, moving, moving.

He reached another glass tunnel. A tall, freckled, crewcut man faced him.

Himself. He caught his breath. Everywhere, mirrors. A small skylight above for ventilation. But no exit that he knew of.

"Alan?"

He narrowed his eyes, located the voice, found that he was staring down a dark corridor that could not have existed.

A figure stood there, motionless. Something glinted in the figure's hand.

"Writers should never run," the voice from the darkness said. "It makes their faces turn red. Take a good look at yourself in one of these mirrors, Alan. You've no idea how ridiculous you look!"

"You lousy bastard!"

Alan's perspective had melted; now, suddenly, it reformed. Until this moment he had not been entirely able to connect the man who had murdered Jess with an ineffectual guy he'd bummed around with. Sure, Paul Bowers had been a whiner and a loser and a neurotic; but, God, not a killer. Killers were what he wrote cheap movies about. Yet—

Alan recalled a book he'd once read for research. A study of criminology. It postulated that every human being on Earth was a potential murderer, needing only the right set of circumstances, the right personal motivation, to turn killer. A world full of dynamite sticks, waiting to be sparked. His engagement to Jess had sparked it for Paul, had set the fuse burning. And it had been burning for a week.

Kid gloves, boy. He's nuts now. You read books on psychology, okay, be psychological. Or, brother, you're dead, too.

"Paul, listen—can't we talk or something?"

The figure did not move. "Clear the air, you mean? Get it all tied up in a neat package?" A small chuckle, like a tapped siphon.

Alan recognized the words, the same words he had used when he gave Paul the straight goods that night. "I didn't mean everything I said. Honest. Is that it?"

"Part of it, Alan."

The blackness stirred. A shape took slow form.

Paul Bowers stepped out of the tunnel, smiling. He was, as always, impeccably dressed. His charcoal gray suit tailored to make him look heavier than his 175 pounds; his shoetips gleaming; his pale, bony face clean-shaven and smelling of lotions. Across his high forehead, the fine blond hair was neatly, perfectly combed. "By the way," he said, "don't try anything dramatic. You're much too clumsy."

He looked white and businesslike and totally unlike a killer, except for his hands. They were powerful, ending in thick fingers; the hands of a longshoreman or a mechanic—or a strangler. In one of them, held firmly, was a twelve-inch blue-steel hunting knife.

Alan looked at it.

"Ugly monster," Bowers said. "But a hunting knife seemed appropriate for the occasion. Borrowed this one from you quite a while ago, if you'll remember. And I thought, 'Now there, by God, would be a touch!' And so it is. At least give me that."

Alan's blood grew hot. "Why did you kill Jess?" he blurted, before he could stop the words.

"The old story, pal. You know: 'If I can't have her, then by the Holies, no one—' Etc. Besides, I wanted to see if I had the nerve. Sort of practice, you might say. For you."

"Paul, listen."

"Of course."

"What do you want me to do? Do you want me to beg for my life, is that it?"

"That would be kind of fun, I must admit. But to tell you the honest to God truth, I'm getting a little tired of the game." Bowers stepped closer, smiling. His eyes were misted over. And the laughter still echoed down the halls.

"You're sick. You know that, I suppose."

"Oh, yes. Mad as a March hare." It was the Party Paul,

the bored intellectual who built his words and rolled them out on oiled casters. "I would describe my illness as Acute Reaction to Prolonged Injustice. The prognosis is fair, however. Fortunately, I know the cure. Jess was part. You, Brother Rat, will complete the treatment."

Alan's throat moved convulsively. In all his films, a man with a knife was a pushover. You kicked it out of his hand, or rushed him before he could use his arm, or bluffed him. But that was the movies. In real life, it worked out differently. A man with a knife was a man with a formidable weapon. If he knew how to use it—and Paul knew—you might as well be in front of a .45 or a cannon.

"Paul, you'll be caught. The police will investigate sure as hell, find we were all friends and track you down wherever you go."

"You really think so?" Bowers lowered the blade, as if bemused by the thought, and Alan stepped forward; but then the knife was up again, and Bowers was laughing. "Alan, you don't give me any credit. You never did, of course." His voice rose in pitch. The smile had become fixed and deadly. "Exactly how long did you think you could go on kicking me before I kicked back, anyway?"

An auto horn bleated out beyond the pier. A strange sound, part of a different world.

Alan remembered the skylight, was very careful not to look up. Was it possible that he could reach it? No. Too high, too small . . .

"I gave you friendship, Alan, and what did I get in return? Betrayal. Oh, I didn't expect you to break your neck trying to give me a little help, but I thought at least you'd appreciate what I'd done enough to stand by me. Not say, 'Thanks, Paul'—no, not that—but maybe show a little loyalty." He was trembling. The hunting knife jumped in short darting flashes in his hand. "Always take, take, take, and never give. Never a helping hand. No; it's good-bye, Paulie, I'm a big man now. Lots of money. Lots of fame. Too busy to help a two-bit loser like Paul Bowers—after I pushed you to the top with my bare hands. Do you deny it?"

"I—"

"Do you deny that it was I who got you in at the studio, introduced you to Kay, almost forced him to hire you? And who was it that stayed up till four every morning helping you to make that lousy script acceptable?"

"I don't argue that you helped me, Paul. I'm grateful for it."

"Grateful!" The thin man drew his lips back. He breathed heavily. "I guess that's what accounts for your aceing me out, playing along with the rumors about, 'Poor old Bowers, all washed up!' And I guess it was the final expression of your gratitude to turn Jess against me?"

"That's a lie, Paul. I—damn it, Jess just fell in love with me. I couldn't help that."

Bowers's jaw muscles twitched. "I believed that for a while, Alan. Felt that maybe I really was the oddball you said I was. But then I started checking around. And I found out a few things. For instance, who it was that talked Kahn into giving me the sack. And who it was that got me blackballed right afterwards." He stepped forward. "I know you pretty well, Alan, enough to know you probably still think of yourself as a noble guy in an embarrassing situation. Those shutters in your mind. They won't let you remember the filthy things you've done."

"It's not true."

"The convenient little shutters won't let you face the fact that you've been scared of me ever since we met. Scared shitless. You know I'd got you in solid at Galactic, so your

189

ego forced you to get rid of me. And it was easy, because I trusted you. I trusted you with Jess, too. All the time you were filling her mind with dirty lies about me, *I trusted you!* And I didn't wake up for a long time. When I did, it was too late. But not too late for me to spoil your little play—"

Bowers raised the knife.

At that instant, Alan grabbed the light bulb in his pocket and hurled it to the floor with all his strength.

The explosion whipped Bowers's head around. In that split second, Alan leapt for the skylight. His fingers closed over the heavy beam, held. Hidden sacs seemed to burst and flood strength through him. A single surge pulled his body up and over the edge. He could feel hands clutching at his legs, slipping, gathering the cloth of his trousers. He kicked, viciously, at the hands, and swung his ankles against the wood. Bowers's hold loosened. He kicked again. The weight fell away.

Alan drew his legs up swiftly, pivoted, and stood up on the slate roof.

Cold bit into his skin; the fog, a wash of wet mist, billowed and pressed in upon his eyes. He balanced there on the slippery roof a brief moment, breathing.

Take it easy, he thought. Try to run and you'll end up cartwheeling off the edge headfirst.

The roof was an iced pond, impossible to run across. Alan squinted. If I could only see! How far down was the pavement, anyway? Where was the edge? He was on a slate island, surrounded by moving gray tides.

And now Paul Bowers's hands were closing over the beam.

Alan crouched above the opening, braced himself and lashed out with his foot. The blow tipped Paul back, forced one hand off. Alan lifted his right foot, prepared to send it heel-down on the strained white fingers.

190

Something grabbed his ankle, jerked.

He caught a glimpse of Paul's face, grinning, blazing red, as though every blood vessel had ruptured and tendriled out.

Then Alan fell.

With a grunt, Bowers heaved through the skylight, landed nimbly, and took the knife from its belt position.

Alan struggled up, his eyes on the long blue sweep of steel in Paul's hand.

"Shutters open, Alan? Or do you still think you're a hero?"

Now!

The blow caught the side of Paul's head, sent him reeling back. Alan felt his muscles go cold: bright color fireworked in his mind. He struck out again, blindly, throwing his entire weight into the blow. Soft inner nose cartilage crunched beneath his hand.

He had not fought for a long time, but now hate activated him, put strength into his arms, goaded him. But even as he swung, he knew that he could never win out against Paul and the knife. Perhaps the blade had already entered his body—they say you don't feel a knife thrust right at first—and his life was, even now, ebbing away.

"Go ahead, Alan, fight! You're doing fine!"

He aimed his fist, drove for that grinning red face. Bone and flesh yielded. But the fury of the lunge pulled him forward. He stumbled, slid, his head striking a ledge of plaster at the roof's edge.

More fireworks. He tried desperately to shake them away. He tried to shake away Paul's burning words, the image of Jess . . . *Was it true?*

Paul Bowers glided toward him, smiling, calm, the knife poised high.

All over now. Done. Finished. He closed his eyes. In a second now. Another second. He waited, his breath in a bottle and the bottle sealed. He could smell the honed steel and the rough leather handle; he could taste the metal in his throat.

A strange sound, then. Like the last drops of water draining from a sink—a short bubbling indrawn scream.

Alan opened his eyes.

Paul had slumped to his knees, teetering, making thin dry noises and staring, staring.

Then he toppled, spilled sideway to the roof, and lay there. His fingers spasmed on the wet slates like the overturned legs of two giant spiders.

Then he was quiet.

In his chest was imbedded the long steel of the hunting knife.

Alan rose, shakily. The roof listed, heaved, settled. A sharp wind from the ocean had cleared some of the fog. Without trying to understand, he located the roof edge again and the pavement below. Less than ten feet.

He jumped. The ground was made of needles and electricity. It buckled his knees. He fell against the rusting ribs of an ancient trolley, and leaned there, trying to swallow.

He began to walk. He listened to the sound of the sea washing in on the beach, and the gulls cloaked high in night, and his footsteps.

Is it true? That was all he could think. He knew that Jess was dead and that Paul was dead and this was no nightmare, no bad dream, but something real; yet, he could only think: Is it true? Did I do those things to Paul, actually, turn Jess against him, actually—

The sky revolved: Alan felt that it had suddenly shaken loose. The peppermint striped shroud covering the Caterpillar began to shimmer and twist darkly; the towering wooden immensity of the Hi-Boy swayed and separated into bright pieces and showered soundlessly down upon him.

He staggered on, out of the amusement park, down a street, to an all-night café. To a phone.

He lifted the receiver off its hook. "Give me the police," he said, in a soft, tired voice.

It was 10 a.m. when they knocked on the door. He'd fallen into a pit of black exhaustion, not bothering to wash or change clothes and getting out of the pit was difficult. When he awoke, he didn't question that the night had been real: his hand ached and his head throbbed and he still felt the numbness.

"Just a minute." His mouth was sour. He could barely remember talking to the police, waiting while they checked his story, staggering out of the squad car.

Alan Cole opened the door. A large man in a brown double-breasted suit stood there. He was flanked by two cops in uniform.

"Yes, what is it?"

The large man stepped inside the room. "A good yarn you told us, Cole," he said. "Mighty good yarn. We swallowed it."

Alan shook his head. This was the man he'd spoken to last night. Captain Boylen, Homicide. But now he looked different.

"What do you mean?"

"Cole," the man said, "you can make it easy, or you can make it tough. It doesn't matter much."

"I—" Alan sat down on the bed; his senses began to swim. "I don't know what you're talking about."

"Then I'll tell you," the man said. "Your story washes out. Point one: We found six bullet holes and a 32.20 at the funhouse. Pistol registered under Paul Bowers's name. We examined the knife. It's yours—"

"I know. I admitted that, didn't I?"

"Then I suppose you know that rough leather won't take prints."

"So what?"

The policeman removed a cigar, skinned off its cellophane wrapping, lit it. "Guy was pretty well armed, wouldn't you say? Gun *and* a knife."

Alan sat quietly, trying to understand.

"Point two," Boylen went on. "We got a report from the medical examiner. It's his opinion Bowers didn't commit suicide. Man decides to kill himself with a knife, Cole, he stabs within an area of a couple inches, like this—" The policeman made stabbing motions against his chest. "There were *four* wounds in Bowers. One here, in the ribs; and here—and here—and finally the one that got him. All spread out. Suicides don't do that, Mister. Care to say anything?"

Alan remembered Paul's telling him of the criminal medicine course he'd taken in Zurich—a course for student lawyers and insurance investigators, the purpose to show the difference between a murder victim and a suicide . . .

"Keep talking, Captain."

"Point three." The policeman removed an envelope from his breast pocket and tossed it over to Alan. "Read it."

Alan removed the letter. Flawlessly typewritten, with thick margins. From Paul, addressed to the police.

"Mailed sometime yesterday afternoon, late," Boylen said. "Downtown got it. Sent it over to me early this morning. Go on, read it."

But even before he began, Alan knew. Everything fell instantly into place. The screwy telegram from San Francisco (*"Sorry it turned out this way. The best man lost. Paul,"*); the shots in the dark and the pistol (to make it appear that they had struggled); the damned hunting knife.

He forced himself to read, knowing what the letter would say, knowing fully.

Homicide Div.
LA Police Department
Los Angeles, California
To Whom It May Concern:

I hope that this letter will end up in your crank files and that I'll wake up tomorrow feeling pretty ridiculous. But for the record—just in case.

I have reason to believe that Alan Cole, an employee of Galactic Pictures, is preparing to do harm to my fiancée, Jessica Randall. Cole and I have been friends for years, and I know him well. He was engaged to Miss Randall up until two weeks ago, at which time Miss Randall confessed that it was I whom she loved and wished to marry. Cole pretended to take it well. But this morning he called Jessica, asking her to have one last drink with him at a little bar they used to frequent, across from Ocean Pier, Santa Monica—Bisco's. I tried to dissuade her from going, but she likes Alan and doesn't feel there's anything to it.

Maybe there isn't. But, as I say, I know Cole. Somewhere inside him, there is definitely a strange and vicious streak. He is a man capable of almost anything.

It's likely nothing will happen. In that case, I'll phone tomorrow. If not, and if this fear of mine turns out to have any justification—contact Alan Cole. But make sure you're armed.

Sincerely,
Paul A. Bowers

Alan folded the letter and put it back in the envelope and handed it to the large man.

"You want to tell us about it, Mister Cole?"

Alan thought of Paul's words, of shutters that would not close inside his mind; of Jess and the clever lies he had told her, unconsciously. The lies he had told everyone, including Alan Cole . . .

Hell of a script, he told himself. Who's the hero? Who's the villain?

"Sure," he said, thinking this was *one* job he wasn't going to ruin for Paul. "I'll tell you about it."

Then he started laughing, and it sounded like the mechanical man at the funhouse. Only he couldn't turn it off.